S0-BBE-235

# THE GIRAFFE

## By Marie Nimier

Translated by Mary Feeney

# THE GIRAFFE

## By Marie Nimier

Translated by Mary Feeney

FRANKLIN PIERCE
COLLEGE LIBRARY
RINDGE, N.H. 03461

**Four Walls Eight Windows,
New York/London**

English translation © 1995 Four Walls Eight Windows
First published as *La girafe*, © 1993 Editions Gallimard

Published in the United States by:
Four Walls Eight Windows
39 West 14th Street, Room 503
New York, N.Y., 10011

U.K. offices:
Four Walls Eight Windows/Turnaround
27 Horsell Road, London, N51 XL, England

First printing April 1995.

All rights reserved. No part of this book may be reproduced, stored in a
data base or other retrieval system, or transmitted in any form, by any
means, including mechanical, electronic, photocopying, recording, or otherwise, without the prior written permission of the publisher.

Library of Congress Cataloging-in-Publication Data:
Nimier, Marie
[Girafe, English]
The giraffe/by Marie Nimier; translated by Mary Feeney.
p.   cm.
ISBN: 1-566858-026-6
I. Feeney, Mary. II. Title.
PQ2674-I 43G5713 1995
            843'.914—dc20                      94-38766

                        CIP

10 9 8 7 6 5 4 3 2 1

Printed in the United States

We wish to thank the French Ministry of Culture and Communication for its assistance in
the preparation of this translation.

There is no great love save in the
shadow of a great dream.

- Edmond Rostand

# 1

The only being in this world I ever loved, I killed. Her name was Solange. Her skeleton is on display at the Museum of Natural History. Thousands of children file by it every year. I know nothing about the investigation that followed her death. It seems to me that no one had a clue. Analysis of her internal organs revealed no trace of suspicious substances, or perhaps there simply was no investigation. Thrilled to come across a perfect physical specimen, science whisked away the body and hushed up the whole affair.

At the time, I didn't know that I loved her.

It all started with a classified advertisement. The Zoological Society was looking for help renovating the exhibit buildings. I was eighteen, just out of high school, and in need of a summer job. With my reserved personality, I wasn't really counting on being hired when I showed up at the appointed time and place. The wan look of the other applicants did little to raise my spirits. There were already quite a few of them lined up in front of the administrative offices. I sat on a step, a little to one side, and hid behind a newspaper. It was the first time I had ever set foot inside the Vincennes Zoo.

After a long wait, the Director in person asked me to follow him into his office. He looked like Noah before the flood, his hands large and knobby, beard straggling over a garnet-red bow tie. His preoccupied manner made me think that the openings had already been filled, and I made no effort to convince him of my special qualifications for the job. I was the thirteenth and last interviewee of the morning; he was probably seeing me out of simple courtesy. I felt idiotic standing in front him, arms dangling, eyes lost in contemplation of a huge goldfish with its limp mouth glued to the wall of its aquarium. I let myself fall listlessly into a trancelike state, I was in uncharted territory, as far removed from everyone else as from myself. Now and then I heard the cries of children, fragile reminders of the outside world.

We stayed that way quite some time—too long—before the Director decided to break the silence. He asked me my name. "Joseph," I answered, and the telephone rang before I could tell him my last name. The line crackled, the Director started shouting that he couldn't talk any louder, he glared at me as if I were responsible for the bad connection. I sneezed, which allowed me to turn away from him in what I thought was a natural way. The room was freshly painted. Roped off with string tied to park chairs in each of the four corners, the blank walls seemed to await visitors to a phantom exhibit. There was nothing to see, nothing more than this glossy surface. The windows at the back of the room looked out onto the elephant exhibit. One of the animals had been observing us from the beginning, rubbing its rump against the grillwork. The Director paced the room, with the telephone cord as a leash. At the ends of sentences, it pulled him back toward the aquarium. His face showed that the person on the other end of the line must be saying something unbelievably stupid.

"I can't be hearing this right," he kept saying, "you're not going to let her starve to death because of some mistake in the paperwork, are you? Just think!"

The conversation I was involuntarily overhearing was becoming heated enough that I thought I should leave, so I slowly backed toward the door. With stunning grace, the pachyderm lifted one of its rear legs and stayed balanced on the other three, stock still. The world could have fallen away. The Director was furiously scribbling a few words on his desk calendar. At that moment I made a break for the door. Just as my hand touched the doorknob, his thundering voice made me jump. "Joseph!" he called curtly, pointing to a Naugahyde bench where I sullenly took a seat. A second elephant came up to the first one; his tusks were crossed in front of his trunk, he had an erection. The size of his organ was impressive. I lowered my head, blushing. Then I heard Solange's name for the first time.

The Director was calm again. "Consider it done," he said. "Our Solange won't have to wait much longer. I'm sending someone right down to you."

I felt him looking at me. Had he noticed my embarrassment? The two elephants clung together. The Director hung up.

"Providence sent you here!" he exclaimed, and since I saw no relation between providence and myself, a small flustered body perched on the edge of a shiny Naugahyde bench, I sneezed. Solange, he explained to me, had just arrived in Marseilles. The health officials there were questioning the authenticity of her vaccination certificate and could not let her out of quarantine without a written release from the Paris Department of Health. Furthermore, the trap door of her cage had warped shut on the ship and the customs officers refused to pry open the hinges themselves. They demanded assistance from a Zoo employee. Since the Pretoria government had sent Solange in exchange for three Charolais bull calves that were supposed to establish the breed in South Africa, things were liable to be blown out of proportion. This deal was part of a larger campaign the Culture Ministries of the two countries were orchestrating, however strangely. The next round would send a troop of baton twirlers from Quimper to Johannesburg—selected, no doubt, for the milky whiteness of their skin.

With these words, the Director flashed a smile at me. Whatever was at stake in this bizarre swap was completely beyond me, so I responded with a quizzical grimace that seemed to please him. After a few terse questions and answers, he asked me if I would be willing to leave for Marseilles to deliver the crucial letter and bring Solange back to Vincennes. If I did, he would keep me on for the summer. I accepted without really knowing what I was signing up for. The terms of the contract were spelled out on the way down the hall: I was hired as a full-time caretaker trainee until the end of September. Two hours later, I was on my way to Orly in an animal wagon. My new job did not seem especially appealing. Little did I realize I would plunge into it body and soul, until it became my whole life.

As soon as I arrived at Marignane Airport, I called my father to tell him I had found work. I had to explain the circumstances of my sudden departure three times before he understood—or, more precisely, pretended to understand—the object of my trip. He thought it sounded shady and warned me about organized crime. When I laughed at his suspicions, he ordered me to get on the first plane home. His reaction made me even surer that the distance between us was more than physical. Having him tell me what to do was like the flick of a finger on a snail's shell. With typical adolescent contrariness I said that I had to hurry to make it to the Port Authority before Customs closed. That did it; I heard him start to mumble. He was lighting a cigarette. I twisted the dial to make it sound like something was the matter with the phone and then hung up. I imagined him, lying on the living room couch in his bathrobe, staring incredulously at the receiver. A cloud of smoke slowly escaped from his mouth. His newspaper slipped to the floor.

Was he really worried? Experience had taught me that nothing could make him act like a father. He pretended; that was the only thing he did well. He treated me like an illness you try to ignore, one of those chronic migraines your friends get tired of hearing about, so you stop mentioning them. He bore his pain stoically; yes, I was his pain. One whole winter I kept leaving a little bent spoon and a lighter in the bathroom without his ever working up the courage to mention it. I accented my natural slenderness by wearing baggy pants and fitted shirts, stopped eating at mealtimes: not a word. Still, I could see he was worried. His cigarette smoking had doubled since we started living together. His inertia made me feel like pounding him. I never missed a chance to let him know. I was disgusted with the way he had let himself go, his body bloated from drinking. His friends were all alike: they talked a lot, in low voices, as if they were plotting something. Some days when I got up to go to school, they would still be there talking around the table. I would stay outside the door listening, hoping to overhear the secrets that kept them up all night, but there was only laughter that sounded like an excuse. When they saw me, something broke in them. They left. Their careful, unsteady footsteps echoed in the stairwell. They could never find the button to push to turn on the hall light. Sometimes they left before I came down, leaving my father dozing in the kitchen, his chin flattened against the back of his hands, his face unguarded. Asleep, he wore the mask of a lost child. His eyelids were so transparent, so thin . . . I loved him too much for it not to matter when I saw him that way, his head like a hunting trophy in the middle of overflowing ashtrays and empty bottles. My father was no good at being alone. I never knew of a woman in his life.

My mother's name was Josephine. A sunny creature from the island of Mauritius, she died of a pulmonary embolism after my birth. I believe that she and my father were already estranged. They had met at the Palace Hotel in Lausanne, through a Swiss dating service specializing in international matches. My father told me this after fifteen years of maintaining that they were introduced at a dinner party in Paris. He was working for an American bank—when he mentioned that part of his life, he always said, "I was still in business." He almost never spoke of my mother. She left me her name, her dusky complexion, dark hair, and fear of drafts. I also inherited a brick-red woolen scarf she had knitted for herself during her pregnancy. All year I wear it wrapped around my neck.

The Director had given me petty cash to take a taxi from Marignane to the Port of Marseilles. When I rolled up the back window, the driver asked if I were cold. In the rear-view mirror, I saw his laughing eyes wink, big drops of sweat beading on his temples. On the plane, they had announced the local temperature, seasonably warm. To cut short any small talk, I answered with an affirmative grunt and slid down behind my scarf. I was beginning to regret taking this job at the Vincennes Zoo. The renovation mentioned in the help-wanted ad would have been preferable to working with animals again. Not that I questioned my skill with animals, quite the opposite: before I moved in with my father in Paris, I boarded with a farm family in Normandy. My adoptive parents kept cows, chickens, a few pigs. I was better with them than anyone, or so the local people said. However, paradoxical as it may seem, I never liked animals—to this day I dislike them. There is something in their way of resembling us that I can't stand. From the time I was a baby, I pushed aside the stuffed animals my foster mother, Mèrade—that was my name for her—regularly gave me for my birthday. I preferred ordinary things: a strainer, a cork, the cover of the butter dish. I had an insatiable need for security, and in these objects I found reliable, discreet companions. They represented nothing other than themselves, and no one made me treat them with the mawkish tenderness you're supposed to display toward a plush bear or panther. I never plunged my little hands into a bunny's fur without feeling an immediate urge to crush it to death against me. Luckily, I could control my impulses around adults. When the family dog followed me, I would wait until we were past the property line before I sent him back. Worse: I would call him—"Malcolm! Malcolm!"—and when he came I would give him a treat, then throw stones at him until he ran away. I enjoyed seeing him thrown into confusion by my conflicting commands. Malcolm was an authentic Norman crossbreed. He looked like a miniature shepherd, with paws too small and a tail too long. All the violence and frustration I felt growing up converged on that poor dog. What could have possessed me to drive him mad? My only excuse was my stupidity, and the state of juvenile confusion that has tormented me ever since. Malcolm was afraid of me, his wariness exasperated me. Obsessed with this animal cunning that eluded my grasp and might betray me, I decided one day to regain his trust. I planned to train Malcolm, I said, and asked to be the only one allowed to feed him. The dog was getting on in years, and I was past the age for childish whims, but even so Mèrade granted my request, thrilled to indulge me for once. It is true that I never asked for anything.

Less than a week without food made Malcolm my friend again. His shifting loyalties reinforced my thinking that he was unworthy of my attention, yet I showered him with care. I spent my whole allowance on treats for him. After school, we would go up in the top of the barn. There, in the semi-darkness, along with his special dog food, I would serve up his daily ration of punishments and rewards. He obeyed me with genuine delight. His servility may have been gratifying at first, but little by little it became as hard to bear as his earlier mis-trust. When he licked me gratefully, I felt like killing him. The odor of his overfed dog's breath, the feel of his rough tongue, his yips of satisfaction, the thin streams of spittle that formed on each side of his muzzle—everything about him nauseated me. Still I let it go on. I put up with his excitement, his whin-ing—and ironically, I felt the tables were turning and I was becoming the victim.

Ripping a teddy bear to shreds and throwing it in the manure pit is one thing, but there was no way I could slit Malcolm's throat without arousing my foster parents' suspicions. Besides, I would never have been able to do it. I was thwarted until I hit on the plan of driving the dog crazy. Over the months I would confine him in narrower and nar-rower spaces, stroking him with one hand and abusing him with the other. When he lay down on his back, paws drawn up on his belly, as if to defend himself from my Machiavellian power, I would fall to the ground and play dead. He would jump up, bend his small head over my face, and bark softly. Malcolm adored me. Once, when I lay there longer than usual, he stretched out full length on top of my body. I felt a wild shock of pleasure. That day I pushed the game as far as it would go. Torn between his overwhelming desire and his fight-or-flight instinct, Malcolm lunged for my throat. I only got two stitches and a dressing I hid beneath my red scarf. I had won. I can still see the desperate gleam in his eyes, and to this day, touching the scar he left gives me strange sensations.

Despite my pleading, Malcolm was declared dangerous and put to sleep. I wished I could save him, sincerely, for I understood that his death would do nothing to free me of him or my complicated reactions to daily contact with animals, a response more difficult to hide with the passing years. I eventually realized that my loathing was too deep-seated not to be the decisive factor in my future.

Fortunately, no one ever suspected. Even the Zoo Director saw me as a fervent animal lover from the moment he interviewed me, no matter how little I did to convince him of the fact. His attitude came as no surprise. For my first fifteen years, I learned to conceal my disdain for the animal kingdom beneath a solid knowledge of its workings. It was probably the only way I had found to gain my foster family's acceptance. Early on, people from the surrounding villages would send for me when a cow was in labor or a sheep was ailing. My ministrations were swift and precise, all the more efficient for being devoid of any sentimentality. No, no one ever guessed what insane torment lurked behind my perfect, too perfect, care. They admired my courage. I was a sickly child, a loner—an image I cultivated. These were the most confused years of my life.

When my father decided to take me back with him in Paris, Mèrade couldn't understand why I was so suddenly removed from her care. Nothing in my behavior had ever betrayed my desire to leave the farm. My adoptive parents had no way of knowing that I was feeding my father horror stories every week, in letters that invariably ended "Aside from that, everything's fine." One day we had slaughtered a pig and my school bag had fallen into the tub of blood, the next day I had to miss school because of a hornet sting on my foot, the next night I woke up screaming when a garter snake slithered out from under my pillow, planted there by the son of the house. I concocted these stories knowing my father wouldn't dare ask for explanations. He faithfully sent a "little check" for my personal expenses, and I thought I detected a variation in the amount according to the  seriousness of the catastrophes I described. I kept copies of my letters and rated them according to the profit they generated. It was simple to establish a list of key elements that opened the floodgates of his guilt—and loosened his purse strings. Slime, darkness, sharp blades were a sure thing. On the other hand, harassment at school and other signs of the covert racism I experienced didn't have much effect on him. Was he ashamed of me? Taunts from the locals only mirrored my father's own distaste for the color of my skin. Unmoved by flights of lyricism, he was easily swayed by the ambiguous nature of my simplest phrases. My main technique was insinuation, suggesting the worst while revealing only the smooth surface of events. I never complained. The spare style I used for burning the midnight oil sold better than anything.

I sent him words, he flung figures back at me. I methodically cultivated my imagination; over the months, the round of daily horrors took shape. The following year, the pace of our exchange picked up. Everything became an excuse for suffering. The least little skirmish was painted as a national disaster. Often, I didn't cash his checks; I was interested in him, not his money. And through him, in myself, no doubt. The process of rating our correspondence—classifying, annotating, sifting through it—provided me with a fairly comprehensive picture of our respective anxieties. Situations that turned my stomach often left him cold. I liked shadows, hidden nooks, solitude. He suffered from claustrophobia. I understood that we were different, which marked a decisive step in the development of my personality. One thing we had in common: the fear of snakes.

Just after Easter vacation, I decided to attack. According to my calculations, I should be able to persuade him that I had to leave the farm before the end of the school year, that it was a matter of life or death. First, I abruptly halted the flow of my letters. A week went by, then two: nothing. I was beginning to have doubts about my strategy when I got a check significantly larger than usual, with a fancy ballpoint pen thrown in. As I had predicted, my father couldn't stand silence.

I was itching to write, my brain bursting with images, and yet I decided not to thank him for his gift. Then, ironically, three weeks into this new regimen I got sick. Really sick this time, despite the doctor's assurances to the contrary. Blood work showed no infectious process, not the slightest anemia. No one was worried, except me. Whenever I tried to stand up, I felt dizzy. I couldn't eat, the mere sight of a bowl of soup turned my stomach. I was jumpy for no apparent reason, I was too hot, too cold, I couldn't get comfortable. I spent hours and hours curled up between two bales of straw in the barn. Malcolm was dead, nothing and no one had been able to replace him. To cheer me up, Mèrade had brought a pair of guinea pigs home from the market for me. One morning I found the female lying lifeless in a corner of the cage. I didn't even have the heart to remove her body. Was the thought of going to live with my father in Paris responsible for my mental state? That was hard for me to believe. I'd been waiting for so long that nothing could hold me back now.

This malaise gradually receded when I began to write again. In addition to my proven methods, I made use of all the emotion stirred up by my body's unexpected revolt. The words flowed from my pen smoothly, sensually. The reason I gave for my silence was an epidemic in the village, an out-break of scoriosis—a disease as dread as it was imaginary—affecting both chickens and adoles-cents for the past few weeks. The high school had been closed. We were already mourning two vic-tims. I didn't specify whether they were in the human or the poultry camp. To stem the tide of panic, local officials had urgently requested that this information be withheld and safety precautions followed to the letter. After begging my father not to breathe a word, I reassured him, saying I swal-lowed a live slug first thing every morning. This pre-ventive treatment had so far proved 100 percent effective. The loach, I explained, or gray slug, secreted a substance found nowhere else in nature. Amazingly tough, it could stay alive two hours after being ingested, conveniently stimulating the needed antibodies. I spared no detail of the loach's delicate descent through the esophagus, then its slow death, dangling from the muscular stomach wall. I signed with an intentionally unsteady hand: "Your son, Joseph." I put my customary "Aside from that, everything's fine" at the bottom of the page, without further comment.

To my great surprise, after my father's death I found all my letters carefully stored in one of his desk drawers. They were filed in order of arrival, unfolded and numbered. Certain phrases were underlined, others corrected or bracketed. We had never discussed my letters, so this discovery touched me deeply. After so many years of ignoring each other, it came as a posthumous sign of his attention. I was beginning to feel guilty about manipulating him when I happened on another file containing a typed copy of each of my tales, plus a section ripped out of some old Yellow Pages, with the addresses of a couple of dozen Paris publishing houses checked off. I noticed that places and dates had been edited out of my letters, and proper names replaced by initials followed by a period, as if to eliminate any speculation that we were related. I was J (period) —Jean, Jacques, Jim?— and he was C (period), an addressee of indeterminate sex, Crab, Crocodile, invisible voyeur and witness to my adolescent ravings. Caught in my own trap, I saw the fantasies of an adventure-starved country boy laid bare on those darkened pages. The truth flew in my face: my father had never believed one word of what I wrote. As usual, he was only pretending. The amount of money he sent was not so much in proportion to his guilt, as I had imagined, but more in response to the quality of my prose. Even today, I shudder to think some third party may have read it all. Out of context, with the inhuman regularity of typewritten characters, it was only a sick and indecent shell of my letters. I burned page after page, not realizing that I was depriving myself of the only link with my past. Still, I can't get it out of my head that I may one day run across this correspondence, published under a pseudonym, mutilated, expanded, in one way or another exploited. I found nothing in my father's personal papers to suggest that his attempts to contact publishers had been fruitful. My library research has turned up no evidence, and now my obsession resurfaces only occasionally. Then I try some new tack. If you really think about it, my letters could only have been published as a series, in a magazine or a specialized publication. That would explain the exorbitant amount of the check he sent to break my silence. My father had probably signed a contract, promised to deliver a new installment every month. I was his ghost, so to speak, and perhaps not the only one.

The scoriosis epidemic and its procession of slimy slugs paid off. How the decision was made I never did learn, but my father magnanimously gave me the use of a sixth-floor walkup servant's room in the apartment building he co-owned. Once I was settled in Paris, I gradually shed my provincial self and became a pimply teenager with no apparent interests. The relief I experienced at no longer having to tend animals quickly gave way to a terrible feeling of uselessness. I was empty and ready to burst, on the verge of bankruptcy. I no longer had any reason to write, my father lived directly below me. It would never have occurred to me to take pen in hand with no particular aim in mind, just out of pleasure, out of need. I spent the month of August holed up in my room, sweating under the covers, convinced that the active life was the moron's way out. That was how I justified the anxiety of those damp nights, the pain of those endless days.

September came, my life found rhythm again—if not meaning. My father had enrolled me in a private school on the rue de Rome. When class was over I would hurry to the train station a block away, the Gare St. Lazare, as if I had someone to meet. That way I didn't have to hang around with my classmates. I discovered the pleasure of melting into the bustle of crowds in transit, and this new mania gave me the strength to go on. It provided almost the same feeling of perpetual imbalance I had found staying in bed all summer. Now, night and day, working around my class schedule, I haunted the vast lobby. I counted my trips back and forth to the snack bar the way a swimmer counts laps. I got so I could distinguish the grinding screech of incoming commuter trains from the creak and groan of main line departures. I navigated by ear. I liked the scent of metal and its bitter, lingering aftertaste.

I was far from the only fan of this anonymous space, but I quickly understood that acknowledging the other regulars was out of place. The next year I hung around Père Lachaise cemetery, and the unwritten rule was the same—to seem like someone just passing through. Keeping your thoughts to yourself, you wander through the tombstones, walk by vending machines, bump into people you recognize but keep your eyes lowered. Becoming transparent is the secret of people who don't want to happen upon their own loneliness reflected in someone else's eyes. I left an old suitcase in a rented locker at the station, taking it out once in a while to give myself an air of credibility—and there was nothing but air inside. I needed to lose myself, invent destinations and appointments. Often I would join a line, the longest one around, tapping my foot as I waited my turn. When it was time to buy my ticket I would break away, running to catch an imaginary train and cursing under my breath. I lived on hot dogs and ham sandwiches wrapped in cellophane I would ball up and hold in my hand for hours. On Sundays, I visited other stations, Lyon or Austerlitz, as a tourist. I would compare them, evaluating size, noise level, crowd density. Despite its unprepossessing architecture, St. Lazare remained —and still remains—my favorite refuge. There I'm on conquered territory, as I was from my very first encounter with Solange.

The taxi smelled of perspiration. After an endless ride, we arrived at the port of Marseilles. The Health Department staff kept me in an airless office for half an hour before they let me near Solange's crate. I had a hard time getting them to take me seriously. One official subjected me to a regular police interrogation before he finally got the Zoo Director on the phone. The partitions were thin and I heard the description he gave of me. I'd never thought I made such a definite physical impression. It took only two sentences to sum me up—and, even worse, for me to recognize myself. Was I really as short, dark, slight as he said? Why did he feel the need to add that even so, I spoke the language fluently? I suddenly felt myself shrink and mat like a woollen blanket dumped in a tub of boiling water, unable to fight off the label so unfairly stuck on me. Dark, thin, and short, that was all there was to me, and nothing in my attitude, the way I talked or moved, could make him forget it.

Finally, it became clear that I was the representative from the Paris Zoo, a very junior representative, to be sure, but still the genuine item, so they owed me a modicum of respect. The man who had phoned the Director asked me to follow him, please, and I stood up, shorter, darker-skinned, punier than ever. Walking through the docks was sheer torture. To keep me going, I tried to imagine the metal framework of the Gare St. Lazare over my head, but on every side there was nothing but water and sky, and the shadeless sun vacationers crave. The ground was going to crumble beneath our feet, boats would capsize, their masts smash to pieces in a tremendous rumble of thunder. My guides strode evenly beside me, untroubled and brisk. Their confident behavior, far from reassuring me, strengthened the sense of imminent catastrophe that washed over me in deadly waves. I have always hated the sea, the smell of it, the sheer expanse. One summer my father dragged me to the seaside, and we spent our time shuttling between the clinic and the pharmacy. I went back to Normandy with a rash all over my body. The family doctor pronounced me allergic to sea spray, I was swabbed with mercurochrome, and there was no more talk of sending me to Le Croisic for my health.

My anxiety subsided once we got inside the warehouses. Boxes were piled all around, the protective ramparts of a greedy, disorganized society. There were tons of misplaced merchandise calmly waiting to be claimed. The man who had made the phone call told me how a shipment of two hundred parakeets had been abandoned the year before. By the time they located the owners—a company with the foresight to file for bankruptcy—the poor cramped creatures had started to eat one another alive. Every morning they had to brave the racket and pull dozens of horribly mutilated corpses out of the bottoms of the cages. I thought of Mèrade's guinea pigs, and to ward off all these terrifying images, I asked the man if he had ever tasted parakeet meat. He looked at me, first alarmed, then puzzled. Unsure whether to take my question seriously, he didn't say another word to me. The deeper we went into the maze of assorted stockpiles, the darker the warehouse got. I thought about the extraordinary field of exploration this stagnant heap would represent for future archaeologists. I often imagine scientists in the post-nuclear universe examining the remains of our civilization. I wonder what strange cult they might reconstitute from the objects of our daily veneration. The day is not so far off when surviving humans will have to dig to discover where they came from, why they are there, clueless, at the head of an army of corpses. Many times I have buried small caches of treasure, hoping that future generations will find the clues to my passage on earth. My father deplored this view of the future, judging it oversimplified and pessimistic. He didn't understand that it was how I dealt with living with him, easing the pain. The temporary state of our existence—the whole human species, not only us on an individual level—made the muddle of lies we lived in seem forgivable. At eighteen, I was already living like a survivor of some disaster, lucky to be alive and determined to keep a grip on things, strapped into an imaginary life jacket that formed a thick wall between me and other people. I was aware of that wall, painfully aware—and I held on tight to the pain.

Our eyes had adjusted to the semi-darkness during the long hike through the warehouses. When we got to the courtyard where Solange was being held, it took me a while to face the sunlight. The crate stood out against the whitewashed wall. It looked huge and black, like an absence of space, a dim and bottomless hole absorbing all the light. Three customs officials were standing guard and I blindly shoved the Director's letter at them. Someone took it, I was introduced by my first name, Joseph, as if that sufficed for someone my age. Three quick handshakes. Then the man who had made the phone call nudged me toward a ladder and told me to go ahead and climb up. There was a small opening in the crate. I stuck my head through it, eager for more darkness. A foul, acid smell flew at my throat. In a fraction of a second, I felt I was reliving the very essence of my childhood on the farm. Something moved, grazing my face. I backed away slowly, overwhelmed by this sweet, moist stench. The feeling was so strong that my body instinctively molded itself to the ladder. I stuck my head back in and stayed still, fingers clenching the edge of the opening. Solange came back toward me. I must have groaned at her touch, and her coat quivered in surprise. I wished that instant could last forever.

A hand grabbed my right ankle, and I felt myself shrivel. Trembling, I brought my head out again and looked down. One of the customs men was pinching his nose.

"Solange is a stinker," he commented with a muffled laugh.

If the others hadn't been there, I think I could have killed him. I decided to try climbing up and prying the door loose.

Ten feet up, the sea was visible. I bashed the wood again and again with a sledgehammer. Solange was stamping the floor of the crate below me. Finally, the hinge gave, and I was so overcome I almost fell. I hunched over. It took all three customs men and then a reinforcement to coax me down.

oting stick, a kind of folding stool
here with him. Heels dug into the
dy bent forward, he looked like a
a jump. The intimate portions of
rubbed the leather seat to shame-
smoothness. The way he strad-
tening to the caretakers' reports
his ambiguous nature to me. I
s inner dialogue by watching how
. He loved women, all women.
ced age, he was suspected of try-
his new hires. According to the
he Zoo restaurant, his taste ran to
generous proportions. I was the
all he desired. I took it very badly
Not that I would have wanted a
him—it would never have entered
e way he played favorites turned
ce I had never attended a coed
ms of attraction and competition
I saw young women as unstable
mysterious preoccupations. I
lking together, and everything
or astonished me. They weren't
foreign to me. How could they
he Director's foolish behavior
ed unworthy of him, and unfair
er his command.
e different. Of course they are
as self-absorbed, but all my life I

## 2

After our two-day journey to Vincennes, first by train, then by truck, I was the only one who could draw Solange out of her crate, across the road, and into her new quarters at the Zoo. She already saw me as her interpreter in these foreign parts. The moment we arrived, the Director summoned me to his office. The paint had had time to dry, but the chairs were still there in the four corners, with string drooping from them. I was relieved to learn that my job description was limited to being Solange's personal caretaker. The head zookeeper would show me the ropes. As far as my schedule was concerned, the Director left me free to work things out with the other caretakers.

Thanks to the head zookeeper's invaluable advice, I quickly had things under control with Solange. I admit the job wasn't especially complicated. The Zoo commissary prepared her food, all I had to do was deliver her meals and clean her cage. I worked almost mechanically, as if to protect myself from her influence. A strange sense of propriety prevented me from acknowledging Solange. She seemed so different from me, at the time, so distant. I preferred to ignore her, she was only an object, the object of my attentions, nothing more.

Only too glad to get away from my father, I worked as many hours as possible. The Zoo staff took me in without really noticing me, to them I was simply a sidekick, the little man in Solange's long shadow. Some of them thought I came from South Africa, didn't even speak their language— and I didn't bother enlightening them. They treated me with a condescending kindness, and when one of them tried to strike up a conversation in halting English, I stared at him with a long-suffering expression. I sensed a flicker of doubt. His smile froze. He stopped trying. That was fine with me. Terrified as I was of reviving my childhood demons, I didn't pay much heed to the people I saw every day. Things went on around me without really registering. The unadmitted purpose of this indifference, I later understood, was to blot out the memory of my feelings the first time I saw Solange on that dock in Marseilles. To blot it out, or perhaps pull it out, the way you pull a weed. For how could I admit to myself that the smell of a dung heap aroused me? How could I explain the desperate rage that took hold of me as I bashed in the door separating me from Solange?

No, it was better to forget. To chalk my state of excitement up to the plane trip, the responsibility suddenly thrust on me. So when I was finished taking care of her, I never stayed around Solange. I walked. I often felt as if I were part of

the scenery
me withou
noticed. N
with their
of the emp
ible curtai
world.

From the
one of tho
to the pati
granted
intended.
cient, logi
The anim
exited at
things rur
was a pa
each per
beast mi
thetical f

The
stories th
were like
classical
employe
veterinar
ence. H
morning
engaged

ever-present sho
that went everyw
ground, upper b
rider heading int
his anatomy had
lessly form-fitting
dled it while lis
quickly revealed
learned to read h
his pelvis moved
Despite his advan
ing his luck with
woman who ran
small minds and
exact opposite of
in the beginning.
relationship with
my mind—but th
my stomach. Sir
school, the proble
were new to me.
creatures with
watched them t
about their behav
frightening, simply
act that way? T
around them seen
to those of us und
Little girls a
just as bold, just

have envied them. The way they acted at the Zoo was one of the things that amazed me most when I started working there. They related to the animals very differently than the adults did. They were more direct, to be sure, but also strangely aggressive. Those first summer days, they wore hand-me-down halter dresses. At the base of the neck, just where the shoulders start, they sometimes had a kind of crease, like the bend of the knee, where the skin was so transparent the veins beneath it stood out. It was a little frightening to sense such fragility. I would probably never have noticed this detail except for the indelible impression one of those little girls made on me. It was a Sunday I'll remember all my life. I was standing at my favorite vantage point, a window in an old storage room above the Guinea baboons' climbing rock. Directly across from me, I saw a man begin to masturbate. It was a fine day and crowds streamed boisterously through the park, but the man seemed completely oblivious. His leather-gloved hand moved back and forth like a forlorn bird, steadily, coldly. His glazed eyes followed the crimson rump of an old female baboon climbing on the boulders. His face was tense, as if caught in a vise of pain. Some Japanese teenagers were clicking photos of the apes, giggling strangely between each snapshot. What did they see through their lenses that we couldn't? Fascinated by the mechanical dance of the cameras, I hadn't noticed a little girl slipping in front of the group. She made a determined path for the man, the back of her curly head right up against his genitals. For an instant he froze, holding his breath, flabbergasted; then, pivoting slightly to the left, he resumed his stubborn pursuit of what was proving a hard-won pleasure.

I was the only witness to this scene, a privilege that left me feeling impotent and guilty. At eighteen, all I knew of love was a few glimpses from my childhood on the farm, when the bull mounted the cows or Malcolm stayed stuck in the game warden's bitch, the least movement causing them to howl like mad. What shocked me most was the little girl's attitude. She seemed to relish the situation, rubbing against the man's legs with oohs and ahs too pronounced to be only for the baboons. Her involvement—discreet at first—became obvious when she began throwing peanuts. She would lean back to take aim, bumping her bare arm against her neighbor's midsection, and as if to excite him she targeted the poor baboons' swollen hindquarters. When she hit one, the little girl would laugh merrily and turn around, looking for a sign of collusion in the man's eyes. But he remained evasive, certainly as disturbed as I was. I think he noticed me, for his hand stopped moving when mine reached inside my fly. I ducked behind the wooden shutters. The man removed his jacket and used it to cover himself. I found him attractive. Form-fitting clothes showed off a long, trim build, an adolescent's body. Only his face expressed a brute strength in keeping with the situation. His short hair accented a huge forehead stamped with crooked wrinkles. Why had he kept his gloves on? I was impressed with the controlled, workmanlike nature of his stroking. Almost involuntarily, I began to copy him, following his rhythm, breathing along with him. I was his invisible mirror, which he must have sensed, since his eyes were glued to the window. From my hideout I saw the whole scene. Encouraged by his daring, I went back to the window. His jacket parted and I saw his skin, white and smooth as a baby's. My last defenses crumbled at the sight of this porcelain fragility. And wasn't his organ much smaller than my own? Noting that fact, childish as it may seem, filled me with uncharacteristic self-assurance. I no longer tried to hide. The girl made strange grimaces, mimicking the apes. Did she see me? I caught her eye, yes, she was watching me, no longer moving, sucking her thumb. Reversing roles, an exasperated male baboon pitched an old bread crust at the crowd. He'd show them. The human hordes jamming up against the bars gave a troubling image of the world outside. What terrifying enemy were they trying to escape? Each person begged for a sign of recognition, and the animals, tired of responding to their ceaseless teasing, resorted to meaningless gesticulations. Only the man and the little girl stood out from the crowd like fireflies in the dark, darting lights in the overgrown weeds along the roads of my childhood. Then everything accelerated: the girl positioned between the two of us, the dual motion of our hands, the girl rocking from foot to foot, our silent straining, the girl . . .

The farmhouse stands at the end of the road, my foster mother is waiting for me on the doorstep, her hair undone. Her husband grabs her from behind, she cries out, I hide behind a bush. She bends forward, what is she looking for? He is strangling her with his strong arms, she tries to get away, she rears, but he holds her tight against him . . .

    The air thickened into a fog and the image disintegrated, leaving me damp, limp, joyless.

When I looked out the window again, the man was gone. I bolted down the stairs, torn between desire and fear, gratitude and disgust. My sticky fingers slid down the railing. I imagined dead sperm cells mixing with dust in the creases of my palm. I was in such a hurry I dropped the keys to the storeroom door in the straw and wasted precious minutes before I found them. Just as I came out, the little girl ran right in front of me. She headed toward a young woman waiting for her, sitting calmly on a bench. The man was nowhere to be seen. I went to the restaurant, hoping it might occur to him to look for me. He wasn't there. I consoled myself with the thought that I never would have dared speak to him anyway. The manager automatically brought me a glass of white wine. The resident tabby cat came to sit on the table in front of me. I scratched his head and he started to purr. It seemed to me that the earth was devoid of humans, that only privileged beings like this, content with anonymous caresses, found life worth living. I thought about my father. The night before, I had found him asleep in the bathtub. The water was cold. Watching him go downhill so fast was more than I could stand. After my third glass of wine, my weariness gave way to a mild state of torpor. Better to take things as they came. I think that the little girl walked by me, hugging a huge stuffed panda, but I couldn't be sure. They all look alike. I got up and walked toward the ticket stand at the Daumesnil Avenue entrance.

The cashier's name was Jeanne Blin. She was the only person at the Zoo whose whole name I knew. Seeing me hesitate one morning about which way to look for the head zookeeper, she took it upon herself to explain the layout and workings of the park. On her map, she pointed out the storage room above the baboon exhibit. They used to keep salt there, she said. With remarkable precision, she gave me an hour-by-hour account of a day in the life of the place that had become her territory in the course of nineteen years on the job. Jeanne knew everyone's schedule to the minute, yet she spent all day stuck in her little wooden ticket booth, with pictures tacked up on the walls. I now think I grouped her with the Zoo's other long-term residents; that was the one and only way I could rationalize visiting her. She was the first animal on the circuit, her booth sandwiched between "tapirs" and "toucans" on the map index. She was trained to sell tickets, count out change, and give soldiers in uniform (up to the rank of sergeant) free admission. The pity I felt for her was completely unwarranted. I wanted to protect her, feed her, stroke her arms. It was ridiculous, no one had ever had that effect on me. Her curly hair, tinted beyond any known color, fascinated me. She was full-breasted, showing off her figure in a filmy white blouse, always the same. I would have liked to be her mother, she could have been mine. Jeanne, Joseph, both five letters starting with J, even our names were alike. I thought it was no coincidence.

I stopped to say hello to her every morning, pleasantly, until that Sunday when I was so upset by the baboon girl that I showed up at Jeanne's ticket booth in the middle of the afternoon, offering no excuse or explanation. I had desperately needed someone who would speak to me as a human being, despite the sperm on the railing, the color of my skin, the three white wines, and the unspeakable desire to see my father's head slowly submerge in the cold tub water. Jeanne Blin did exactly what I expected of her. She asked what was new with me, complained about the heat, said it was a shame about Li-Li, the male panda donated by Mao Zedong and now dead of a pancreatic tumor. She almost wept telling me how Yen-Yen, his mate, would be all alone. I listened, leaning against the cash register, feeling good. For a moment I thought we were going to become real friends. When she bent down to pick up a coin that had fallen on the floor, I stretched over the counter. I took a closer look at a postcard tacked to the back wall. It was a picture of a weather-beaten cabin by a blue lake ringed with mountains.

"Norway," she declared solemnly, as if introducing an important member of her family.

"How do you do?" I replied with a small bow.

It wasn't meant to be funny, but Jeanne laughed. It was the first time in ages I had made someone laugh aloud. People might chuckle, but they never seemed to know quite what to make of me. I cracked my jokes at the least likely moments, never changing my expression, and nobody got them. At any rate, when I bowed to Norway, I managed to sneak a peek at Jeanne's legs, just out of curiosity. That was when I saw the Director's shooting stick propped up in a corner. It took my breath away. Then I spied his garnet-red bow tie. Yes, his trademark pre-tied tie, I was certain, poking out from behind the striped curtain, at the cashier's feet. I thought I would never be able to tear my eyes away; my head swam with frightful images. Jeanne laid a hand on my shoulder and I sensed her trying to nudge me backward. I resisted. She brought her painted mouth close to my ear, as if about to whisper a dirty joke, and asked me to go buy her a packet of tissues. "Hay fever," she explained, pressing harder with her hand. I didn't move. This resistance gave rise to a peculiar pleasure. I thought of Malcolm. Near the picture of Norway another postcard was tacked up; this one was from Rome, the she-wolf at the Capitol suckling Romulus and Remus. The bronze gleamed like sweaty skin in the sun. I straightened up and marched off without another word.

When I returned with the tissues, the front panel of the booth was pulled down. I left them on the bench across from it and went back to my lookout in the storage room. The baboons were resting up from their busy Sunday, huddled together in a cranny. The day's last visitors didn't stop to linger in front of the cages. Soon the Zoo would close its gates. Would my father be expecting me for dinner?

I never did find out whether the Director was really there, crouching behind the striped curtain. To judge from how solicitous the cashier was the next day and for days afterward, I would say my suspicions were more than the product of my imagination. She offered me coffee from the cap of her Thermos and asked me a flurry of questions about my past. Did she think that if I confided in her, she'd gain my cooperation? I made up stories and told them with dubious conviction. My silence was not for sale, Jeanne would have understood that if she were really my friend, and her much-older husband's fits of jealousy—he was, after all, a married woman—were of as little interest to me as my Normandy childhood was to her. My disappointment deepened with each of my visits. I vowed I would stop going to see her, but something pulled me irresistibly to her booth every day. Although Jeanne's conversation often annoyed me, I couldn't go without seeing her. I needed to hear her slightly flat voice trail off at the ends of sentences, like a tulip wilting. Eventually I saw that it was only the idea of my not being with her that bothered me. What did she do when I wasn't there? And why on earth didn't her knitting go any faster?

I had been at the Zoo seven weeks when the conversation worked its way around to the theme of love and betrayal. Jeanne Blin lit up, her eyes had a gleam I had never seen in them. She spoke nostalgically of her first romantic encounters as a teenager, concluding that even today, her feelings were the same. I don't remember how it happened, but I recall the exact moment I decided to break up her affair with the Director. The sky cleared suddenly. Though Jeanne was still animated, now she left me cold. Did she realize my attitude had changed? She fell silent. I smiled at her. Jeanne smiled back. I was already concocting the plans for a terrible blackmail that would send her life into a tailspin, and drag me down along with it. A strange sense of pride fills me when I go over it all in my mind, though I know I should feel ashamed.

I use the term blackmail, but I just kept an eye on Jeanne's ticket stand. To my amazement, not one day went by that the Director didn't spend some time with her inside the booth. He chose times when it was slow, she closed her wooden shade . . . If a visitor wanted a ticket, she would send him over to the main entrance. Once some-one wouldn't take no for an answer, and the cashier's hand poked through the wooden slats, a flesh-and-blood Jack-in-the-box with painted nails, pinching an entrance ticket between the thumb and index finger. This apparition made me sick. The trapped wrist, the redness of her skin, the way she dispatched one portion of herself to serve the out-side world, while inside the booth she gave the rest of her body to the Director, plunged me into a world of dread. Up to that point, my plan to break them up had been a kind of game; now it shifted dramatically. I could not bear to live with that image in my mind, it disgusted and revolted me, the only way to free myself was to destroy it. I mustered all the strength necessary to conquer my scruples— and my shyness. When I saw them emerge from the booth, Jeanne looking misty, the Director trembling, a surge of hatred for the two of them jolted me. After looking both ways, as if crossing a dangerous intersection, the cashier trotted off toward the rest rooms. The Director lingered by the vulture exhibit, lost in contemplation of the shredded meat left on the huge bones dangling in the branches. A bird with a featherless neck perched in front of him and spread its broad wings. Finally, the Director headed back toward his office. Did he sense something? One last time, he turned back toward the booth.

From that afternoon on, I decided not to let the cashier out of my sight unless it was Solange's feeding time, even if I had to finish my work before the Zoo opened or after closing. There was no way Jeanne and the Director could meet. Jeanne didn't seem to mind. If my constant presence irritated her, she didn't let on. With her lips soft and smooth as the skin of a fruit, she continued to dig into my past. When she arrived in the morning, her face still rumpled with last night's dreams, I was waiting at her doorstep. Then I would go buy her a croissant or a brioche, she'd take out her thermos, and we would share a second breakfast. Toward lunchtime, the Director would sometimes steal by, but I was still there next to the cash register, tearing tickets, like a rock. When Jeanne counted down her cash drawer just before closing, I counted along over her shoulder. I learned to roll change and sort bills in staggered piles of ten. I was her escort to the accounting office when she turned in her receipts. Not caring if my co-workers gossiped, I didn't leave her side until we reached the steps down to the Porte Dorée subway stop. She disappeared down into the dark and I walked back to the Zoo. When I passed his office window and happened upon the Director, his waxen face bent over his papers, shut inside his four impeccable semi-gloss walls, that was the one moment I felt happy. I had kept them apart one more day. I had absorbed the attraction between them and turned it against them, I strained against their passion, they belonged to me in a way. So I measured the true meaning of the verb "to possess." I began to sense that the drama I had acted out with Malcolm was only the dress rehearsal for what would become my life. I rejoiced in calculating the number of rendezvous between the Director and the cashier I had managed to thwart. But my euphoria was short-lived, and when I was back in my one small room, the fear of losing, failing, brought all my uncertainty home to me. What would happen if they made plans to meet over the weekend, or some evening, outside the Zoo? The only way around that possibility was to arrange the terms of their next meeting myself. In any case, I couldn't maintain this state of siege indefinitely. Even when I concentrated on the memory of the hand sticking out between the wooden slats, Jeanne's incessant questioning exasperated me. I couldn't even take her coffee anymore. Her kindness made me anxious.

And what if her hidden desire was to have me replace the Director, on the shooting stick, behind the wooden blinds?

I had never dared look inside the booth during their revels, but I know today that my imagination went beyond reality, far beyond. The idea of finding myself shut in there with the cashier, alone and naked, was what I liked to think about most. Many sleepless nights I mulled over our bodies, and our words, those words we would surely have to say before embracing; I knew neither how to say them nor what they meant. That bothered me the most: I lacked a vocabulary. The pornographic movie I forced myself to sit through at a triple-X theater near the Gare St. Lazare was no help at all in the matter. I have only a jumbled memory of the film. The women, and their strange way of parting their legs in closeup, left me perplexed. Their mewing cries came out of the loudspeakers like the semen from the men's pricks, in unpredictable spurts, and I couldn't begin to understand what was at the bottom of their pleasure. I was mired in speculation. Nothing in the whole experience made me hard; I felt as if something were missing in me. My notions of female anatomy may have become more precise, but the nature of human attraction eluded me. I was forced to admit, even if the idea disturbed me, that the only way to satisfy my curiosity would be to witness a real-life love scene, with no panning or fade-outs. So, after two weeks of surveillance, I decided to send the cashier and the Director flying back into each other's arms.

The date was set for the day of the next staff meeting, thanks to two copies of a supposedly anonymous message composed with words cut out from various magazines. I had resorted to this rather quaint method less out of real necessity than a desire to create an atmosphere of mystery around the lovers' reunion. I believe my lead actors wanted it so badly that they would have followed any directive, even one in my own handwriting. Sealing the envelopes, I thought about the letters I sent my father. I often used to keep them in my book bag for several days before mailing them. I liked the looser feel it gave the paper. I also liked the calculated shakiness of my handwriting. It was scratchy and crooked, as if I had written in secret, in the beam of a half-dead pocket flashlight. I saw myself biting my pen, completely absorbed in the blank surface where everything was possible, everything except chance.

Behind Solange's cage, between the feed room and the outer pen, were two old artists' lofts. I had arranged for the cashier and the Director to meet there. Invisible to the public and animals as well, the studio windows looked out over the giraffe exhibit and a part of the restaurant. That way the artists could observe their models in perfect safety, without being distracted by curious visitors. Jeanne herself had pointed the small rooms out to me on her map, with the tip of her knitting needle. The studios had fallen into disuse once photography became the rage. They had not been maintained, and very few Zoo staffers even remembered they were there.

The stairway was still in very good condition despite the leaky roof, and all it took to pry open the door was a bit of wire and a screwdriver. Upstairs, the space was divided into two adjoining studios. The first one seemed suspended in time: the painter would be back in a moment, his work must have been interrupted suddenly, for his tubes of paint lay there uncapped. Besides his painting gear, the artist had brought in a cot, two chairs with straw seats, and a crate piled with old books. The painting in progress stood backwards against the wall, and some obscure compulsion kept me from turning it around. A picture of the Virgin Mary was stuck on the back of the frame. Adding to the eeriness, a dozen brushes dangled on nylon string from the ceiling; they floated in space like so many drunken birds frozen in mid-flight. Their pointed beaks were ready to light into the empty easel, a shield standing firm on its three wooden legs. A weird mosaic of splotches covered the terra cotta floor tiles. Despite the thick coat of dust on the palette, it was easy to pick out burnt sienna, red ocher, sand. I thought of Italy, the warm hues of the houses, the

streets deserted on hot afternoons. I had never set
foot outside France, but for me that was what Italy
looked like. A big hazy mirror reflected the window, a pale and flickering light shone on the thick
curtain separating the two studios. The room on the
other side was completely bare, without one scrap
of cloth or speck of paint. The contrast was so
strong that even the air inside seemed tangible, like
something full and heavy.

The morning of the big reunion, I moved the cot
into the empty studio and made an invisible slit in
the folds of the curtain. I can still picture myself sitting there on a chair, my back straight, throat tight.
I don't think I would have been any more nervous
waiting to jump off a cliff. The cashier arrived first
and I almost bolted when I heard her footsteps on
the stairs. But no, I stayed put, paralyzed, my heart
pounding. She paused on the landing, then I heard
the door of the empty room open. She entered my
field of vision in fragments, first from the back, then
the side. She was wearing a white skirt that day to
match her standard blouse. I had made sure the
curtain was securely fastened to the wall, but I was
too familiar with her insatiable curiosity not to
worry that she might try to investigate. Fortunately,
she headed straight for the bed. She set down her
purse, extracted a rubber disc, and smeared it with
cream. Then she inserted it beneath her clothing, a
blank expression on her face. Arching her back-

side, she concentrated for a few seconds, then relaxed her body and withdrew her hand, frowning as she sniffed it. Her skirt caught in her belt for a second and I saw that she was wearing thigh-length stockings that apparently stayed up on their own. The skin just above the nylon looked red and oily. The cashier inspected the bedspread. She sat on the edge of the cot, lacing her fingers over her knees. Then the two of us waited.

Finally, the Director arrived. Without even greeting Jeanne Blin, he barked that the staff meeting started in seventeen minutes. He took out his pocket watch, flipped it open, and corrected: "Sixteen minutes, exactly sixteen," to which she replied with a worried look: "Then let's hurry."

I was flabbergasted. My dream was to observe a true lovers' rendezvous, with its own special language and customs, so this exchange was like a slap in the face. I thought they would probably start laughing, that they were only pretending, but no, the small talk ended. Then they were on each other so fast I couldn't quite figure out how the cashier wound up on her knees, her blouse unbuttoned to the waist, both hands kneading our boss's crotch.

A few minutes went by—precious minutes before we were due at the staff meeting. The Director was overheating by the time he unfolded his shooting stick. So my hunch about its connection to his sex life was on the mark! His pants slid down to his ankles. The cashier nimbly unhooked her bra. She was really taking the job in hand. I stood up to get a better look. Freed from their cage of lace, her breasts flopped like rag dolls. This nonchalance was not without beauty. She was facing me and her features told me the words she couldn't say. In her clear eyes, I saw tenderness, discretion. I pitied her. Still, she boldly met her lover's impetuous demands: now he rubbed his half-limp organ against her breasts, her stomach, between her painted lips. A streak of red trailed across the smooth and powdered skin of her cheeks. Although deep down such violent desire aroused me, it also made me feel embarrassed, for despite their attempts at passion it was clear that their bodies, or minds, weren't in completely in synch; something I couldn't quite name was missing.

"Jane, Jane . . . "

Still standing, with his pants and now his shorts twisted around his ankles, his coccyx riveted to the tawny leather seat of the shooting stick, the Director pulled her to her feet, pulled Jane, as he now suddenly called her in English, plaintively, and made her mount him. But her name isn't Jane, that's ridiculous, I wanted to shout, to make him stick to the truth. "Jane," he sighed as he shoved his weary prick into Jeanne, the French cashier, with her stockings still miraculously in place, her gooey rubber disc and her old husband waiting at home.

She moaned. How could she be enjoying this shameful masquerade? He turned purple when she took his thumb, then his index finger, into her mouth and sucked on them. His face swung toward me, features were frozen in a horrible grimace. A strand of his beard between his teeth, his pupils dilated, the Director suddenly stopped breathing. His neck was thrown back and over the elastic band of his bow tie spread twin rolls of flesh that bristled with gray hairs. I thought he had lost consciousness when the cashier began to cry no, no, clasping him to her. Panicking, I ran to the studio window to call for help, knocking into the dangling paintbrushes and sending them twirling around the easel. One of them caught on my scarf and it was a moment before I could pry loose from its lifeless grip. Then, framed in the window, Solange's small head appeared.

There was such trust, such curiosity in the way she came to look at me, that I felt a lump in my throat. I approached slowly. Warm breath fluttered on my forehead. Her eyelashes were huge, and her dark almond eyes stood out against her amber coat. They spoke of the intelligence, the delicacy, the divine grace of shared silences. That was where true happiness lay, not in the grotesque antics I had unwittingly orchestrated for an audience of one. When I raised my palm to her muzzle, she shied and backed away, still staring at me. I swore I would teach her to accept my caresses. And to desire them.

"Who's there?"

The Director wasn't dead after all. His voice came from behind the curtain, but I understood from his tone that if I didn't act fast I'd soon find myself face to face with him. I grabbed the painting propped against the wall. Behind this makeshift shield I flew down the stairs, slammed the door behind me, and threw the bolt. The latch came off in my hand; I tossed it into the bushes. It would take the Director a while to force the lock. No one had seen me leave. I walked deliberately toward the inner galleries, heading for my hideout in the old storage room. When I finally looked at the painting, still quaking with fear, I understood that my encounter with Solange was not mere chance. The subject was a young giraffe and its keeper— not surprising, considering the location of the studios. The two of them stood in a welter of sketchy landscapes that appeared piled one on top of the other, making it hard to figure out exactly what story the background was telling. One detail caught my eye: a swath of brick red that seemed to be the focal point of the whole composition. It was a big ribbon around the giraffe's neck, the exact shade of my beloved woollen scarf. Hanging from it was a small box that must have contained some talisman against the evil eye.

At the bottom, the painter had traced the title

of his work in fine calligraphy: "The Pasha of Egypt's Giraffe and Her Keeper Yussef." In the center stood a swarthy man wearing a long khaki robe. His right hand clenched the end of a baton slipped inside his sash. His black eyes shone with a supernatural light.

50 • Marie Nimier

# 3

Yussef rode ahead, so he was the first to spy the long, long neck emerging from a grove of acacias—the neck of their prospective victim. The body, perfectly still, was lost in the interwoven branches, tail sweeping flanks with machinelike regularity. How could nature have made such a blatant mistake? For despite her desperate attempts to blend in with the landscape, the giraffe stuck out. She appeared planted there by a divine hand, an incongruous scenic overlook in those parched and thorny valleys.

Atir began shouting in his harsh voice, ordering the hunters to circle the grove. No one liked him, yet everyone heeded his commands. His ambition was fascinating. Alarmed by the noise, the giraffe bolted out of the trees. Then Yussef understood why she had waited so long to flee: a yearling calf scrambled to keep up with her. Was it sick? The calf's neck swayed left to right, as if to say it was too late, too late. Sure enough, Atir caught up with it. He was about to raise his weapon when Yussef stopped him with a snap of his whip.

"We'll bring it back alive," he announced.

Upon which, he twirled his homespun cloak around in the air like a lasso until it landed over the head of the terrified calf. Atir, furious at being thwarted, stormed off, swearing, in pursuit of the mother.

Killing an animal was considered a collective act of love, with its courtship phase, its code of behavior: a peerless way to take a man's measure. Yussef hated these barbarian customs. He alone resisted the horrible pleasure of watching the mother giraffe, her four tendons sectioned, slowly sink down and impale herself on Atir's lance. She kept breathing for a long time. The overexcited hunters savored their victory inch by inch; with the animal's every movement a hoarse, involuntary cry went up. Her neck stretching toward the grove of acacias, eyes bulging, the giraffe took forever to die. Not the slightest sound came out of her gaping mouth.

The calf was tied to a tamarind bush and the mother was butchered on the spot. Everyone loaded his share of bloody meat on his camel as best he could; then the evening meal would begin. A prize cut had been set aside to celebrate this double capture. The grilling meat gave off an acrid smell that rhythmic fanning with palm fronds failed to dispel. The air remained hot and heavy though night had fallen. A goatskin full of water was emptied over the dead giraffe's eyelids. That way her soul would drown and never come back to trouble the sleep of the living. According to a tradition handed down from the ancient Egyptians, the head was buried at the exact spot of the kill. Thus ended a life as harmless as it was useless.

Yussef kept his distance from the fire and the feast. As he was the close friend of Mouker Bey, the governor, the men had awarded him the giraffe's tail. The black hairs of the tuft would fetch a fortune at the Sennar bazaar; they were said to protect against lions and unfaithful wives. Yussef had also retrieved two stripped tibias no one else wanted.

With the flat of his knife, he cleaned the first thigh bone and hung it from his sash like a sword. Then, in one diabolically precise stroke, he slashed off the head of the second bone. A white substance spurted out and Yussef cupped it with his lips, flicking his tongue into the hollow of the bone. He sucked in the warm, thick sap, held it a few seconds against his palate, taking care not to mix his saliva with it, then spit it out into his left hand. Making sure no one could see him, he plunged the hand between his brown thighs and furiously worked the marrow into the deepest recesses of his being. Ashamed, he covered both hands with sandy soil and fell asleep.

Yussef awoke before the others, with an empty stomach and a muddled mind. The decapitated tibia lay a few inches from his eyes. He wanted to grab it and fling it away from him, but his hand froze. The bone seemed to throb with an inner life. Was it really moving? Thinking it was a hallucination, Yussef shook his head. Some strange force prevented him from getting up. That was when he saw hundreds of scarab beetles teeming at the open end of the bone cavity, or perhaps not scarabs but another greenish-shelled insect he didn't know by name. They were fighting their way in, trampling each other; a few, smothered beneath the swarming mass, helplessly attempted to back out. Filled with panic, Yussef hugged his knees to his belly, as if to save himself from some terrifying invasion.

Long minutes went by before he could tear his eyes away from the battle scene. Finally, rousing from his stupor, he backed away, then made a break toward the camels. Out of breath, he filled a basin with milk and sprinkled himself with it. The purifying liquid ran down his legs. He drank some, too, and it was only then that he realized he had to feed the young giraffe. He started milking again, calm now.

Walking through the camp, he noticed the insects had not attacked the leftover food. He picked out some flat bread, beans, a few dates. Atir snored by the fire, legs spread, arms crossed beneath his head. His face tensed with every breath he took. His nostrils were surprisingly mobile. Yussef smiled at the idea of looking for the beetle-infested bone and setting it down by his enemy. The young giraffe was sleeping, gracefully curled up. Its rosy coat seemed to reflect the sun's first rays. Yussef stayed watching the calf a long time.

It was only a short distance from the storage room to the restaurant, where the staff meeting was being held in the back room. Reluctantly, I found a hiding place for the painting of the giraffe and Yussef, her keeper. I could have looked at it for hours.

From the waves of noise cresting out of the restaurant's big bay windows, I could tell that the Director had not shown up yet. This was the first time I had seen the whole staff assembled, and I was amazed at the number of people I didn't recall ever noticing, either in the exhibits or the administration buildings. It is true my powers of observation had been blunted since I began caring for Solange. Or, rather, they had become so concentrated that I would focus on the most insignificant details: a button missing on a jacket, the length of a pant leg, a hand with dirty nails, a bracelet, a bruise. I spent so much energy on concealment— acting, walking, thinking, living on the sly—that things now concealed themselves from me, which was becoming hard to reconcile with the demands of the job. My supposed South African background was beginning to wear thin as an excuse. Although my assignment was quite simple, and limited, I was supposed to work as part of a team, and here I could barely manage to remember my co-workers' faces, let alone their names. I tried to tell them apart as best I could by the color of their uniforms. To compensate for this failing, I pleaded myopia— recurrent attacks of temporary nearsightedness, a condition inherited from my father, I explained to the cashier when she expressed surprise at the sudden shifts in my behavior. When someone spoke to me, I squinted and walked right into him, like the

Director's goldfish bumping against the walls of the tank. In the most extreme cases, I would pull a big pair of glasses out of my pocket and carefully slide them up my nose, almost past the bridge. Then I wasn't pretending anymore: everything was a blur, the other person's pimples disappeared. Behind my thick lenses, I could say anything, without worrying about possible consequences. I felt my body flow into this gelatinous mist effortlessly, gracefully as a drop of oil falling into a glass of water. Blindness set me free. No longer a slave to outward forms, I finally became myself.

I have never fully understood how such an inconsequential accessory allowed me to distance myself so thoroughly from the impression I made on others. Nevertheless, I employed this subterfuge with ease and at times even a certain sensual pleasure. I enjoyed seeing shapes blur together, faces collapse, until things blended into a vibrating mass of colors. The fact that a person standing in front of me could be so suddenly transformed into a sickening blob made me think about the illusory nature of our perceptions and what we pompously call reality. I felt I was gaining access to another type of data. In fact, I owed my discovery of the affair between Jeanne Blin and the Director to my myopia. Otherwise, why would I have bent closer to the postcard of Norway? Since my vision had always been excel-

# 2

After our two-day journey to Vincennes, first by train, then by truck, I was the only one who could draw Solange out of her crate, across the road, and into her new quarters at the Zoo. She already saw me as her interpreter in these foreign parts. The moment we arrived, the Director summoned me to his office. The paint had had time to dry, but the chairs were still there in the four corners, with string drooping from them. I was relieved to learn that my job description was limited to being Solange's personal caretaker. The head zookeeper would show me the ropes. As far as my schedule was concerned, the Director left me free to work things out with the other caretakers.

Thanks to the head zookeeper's invaluable advice, I quickly had things under control with Solange. I admit the job wasn't especially complicated. The Zoo commissary prepared her food, all I had to do was deliver her meals and clean her cage. I worked almost mechanically, as if to protect myself from her influence. A strange sense of propriety prevented me from acknowledging Solange. She seemed so different from me, at the time, so distant. I preferred to ignore her, she was only an object, the object of my attentions, nothing more.

Only too glad to get away from my father, I worked as many hours as possible. The Zoo staff took me in without really noticing me, to them I was simply a sidekick, the little man in Solange's long shadow. Some of them thought I came from South Africa, didn't even speak their language— and I didn't bother enlightening them. They treated me with a condescending kindness, and when one of them tried to strike up a conversation in halting English, I stared at him with a long-suffering expression. I sensed a flicker of doubt. His smile froze. He stopped trying. That was fine with me. Terrified as I was of reviving my childhood demons, I didn't pay much heed to the people I saw every day. Things went on around me without really registering. The unadmitted purpose of this indifference, I later understood, was to blot out the memory of my feelings the first time I saw Solange on that dock in Marseilles. To blot it out, or perhaps pull it out, the way you pull a weed. For how could I admit to myself that the smell of a dung heap aroused me? How could I explain the desperate rage that took hold of me as I bashed in the door separating me from Solange?

No, it was better to forget. To chalk my state of excitement up to the plane trip, the responsibility suddenly thrust on me. So when I was finished taking care of her, I never stayed around Solange. I walked. I often felt as if I were part of ever-present shooting stick, a kind of folding stool that went everywhere with him. Heels dug into the ground, upper body bent forward, he looked like a rider heading into a jump. The intimate portions of his anatomy had rubbed the leather seat to shamelessly form-fitting smoothness. The way he straddled it while listening to the caretakers' reports quickly revealed his ambiguous nature to me. I learned to read his inner dialogue by watching how his pelvis moved. He loved women, all women. Despite his advanced age, he was suspected of trying his luck with his new hires. According to the woman who ran the Zoo restaurant, his taste ran to small minds and generous proportions. I was the exact opposite of all he desired. I took it very badly in the beginning. Not that I would have wanted a relationship with him—it would never have entered my mind—but the way he played favorites turned my stomach. Since I had never attended a coed school, the problems of attraction and competition were new to me. I saw young women as unstable creatures with mysterious preoccupations. I watched them talking together, and everything about their behavior astonished me. They weren't frightening, simply foreign to me. How could they act that way? The Director's foolish behavior around them seemed unworthy of him, and unfair to those of us under his command.

Little girls are different. Of course they are just as bold, just as self-absorbed, but all my life I the scenery. I was a perch, a rock, people looked at me without seeing me, I observed without being noticed. My favorite visitors strode through the zoo with their hands in their pockets, stopping in front of the empty cages. They were searching. An invisible curtain separated them from the rest of the world.

From the first, it was obvious to me: the Zoo was one of those magical places that reveals itself only to the patient and the discreet. Anyone taking it for granted would see no more than what was intended. Everything would seem shipshape, efficient, logical, and in a sense that would be correct. The animals were fed, the public entered and exited at the appointed times, work crews kept things running smoothly. And yet, behind the bars was a parallel world of barbaric poetry, where each person was a solitary agent, where man and beast mingled on this ark waiting for the hypothetical flood.

The Director ran the ship with an iron fist. The stories they told about him in the Zoo restaurant were like legendary episodes in the tale of some classical hero. At the time, he hand-picked all his employees, from the groundskeepers up to the head veterinarian, which gave the staff mysterious coherence. He knew all of us by our first names. Every morning he went on his rounds. As soon as he engaged in a conversation, he would straddle his because I could see and comprehend them. I thought of Malcolm, the baboon man, the letter campaign that brought me back to Paris, and everything seemed to be leading to that precise instant at the table with an empty glass in front of me, when I decided to dedicate myself completely to my strange calling.

Lost in my daydreams, I didn't notice the room slowly emptying. The Director's compulsive punctuality was an essential component of his public image, so his lateness made his staff worry. He wasn't in his office, or with the big cats; none of his close associates had seen him for over an hour. The head zookeeper had just come back from his rounds on his ancient black bicycle. He hadn't noticed anything out of the ordinary. To everyone's surprise, he headed straight for my table. He asked if I knew where Madame Blin was, and when I said I didn't have the foggiest idea, he took me by the arm and led me outside. The alcohol made me less tongue-tied than usual. Cool as a cucumber, I told him how the cashier had deserted her post, and me, thirty-five minutes before closing time. I liked the head zookeeper. Behind his clear blue eyes I sensed the rotting monster that gnawed away at his life. He seemed to be constantly reinventing the world, as if to block out a painful past. He now listened to me so intently I couldn't resist a little more storytelling. When I kept pestering the cashier with questions, I explained, she got mad. I had trailed her to the rock above the giraffe exhibit, but she got away when I stopped to direct a visitor to the rest rooms.

I paused for effect. The head zookeeper thought I was hesitant to go on in front of the others. We stepped slightly to one side, and as clearly as I could so everyone would notice, I pointed toward the studios.

"I'll bet she went up there for a rest," I added.

"And the Director," he asked in a quieter tone, "you wouldn't know . . . "

I shrugged, as if to say I'd done all I could to prevent the inevitable. I motioned toward the rock again, more discreetly this time. The head zookeeper leaned closer.

"I really don't see where else . . . " I concluded after a long silence as I brushed against him. His uniform smelled like the country. I dragged my unfinished sentence out shamelessly and shook my head in disapproval. I noticed his shoes were well past needing a shine. At that moment my glasses— the ones without lenses—fell to the ground. Why had the optician insisted I buy them so big? The head zookeeper bent to pick them up. I snatched them out of his hands.

"An accident," I stammered, "I sat on them this morning, broke the lenses . . . stupid of me, ha! ha!, they broke in a million pieces."

The head zookeeper stared at me in surprise as I mumbled more excuses. "No harm done," he kept saying. Despite his kindness, I couldn't calm down. I started searching for my other pair of glasses, the ones with lenses, as if to prove I really was nearsighted, he had to believe me. Then the Director's voice, amplified by the echo in the boulders, came roaring out, and I latched on to it like a drowning man clutching at a life preserver.

"Jane," he called, "Jane, we can get out now, I broke the lock."

The sound came from the exact spot I had pointed to a few seconds earlier.

"You see," I burst out, "I wasn't lying to you, was I?"

I finally found my glasses. The head zookeeper's face blurred and I managed to get control of myself. The knot of employees around me tightened. Straining our ears toward the same precise point in space, we listened for Jeanne's reply. When it didn't come, someone suggested drinking a round to the Director's health, but the crowd remained silent. The small group of groundskeepers wandered away, as if the whole affair was none of their business. The vast majority of the staff had no idea the studios were even there, and we couldn't see the screened windows from where we stood. You could tell from the way they scrutinized the rocky wall that they were expecting their boss to appear on the wooden ladder leading down from the feed room, disheveled, his beard full of straw and bow-tie dangling miserably from the notch in his collar.

The head zookeeper, despite his imposing build, watched things unfold naively as a child. I admired the formidable capacity for wonder in this man nearly three times my age; I envied him. He was like his bicycle, solid and efficient, simple like things from the olden days, as they're called. How much did he know about the cashier and the Director? Every morning at eight he went around to collect each animal keeper's daily report, so he knew a lot about what went on. He transmitted the news of the day from one exhibit to the next, and if he sometimes spoke out of turn, it was always with such candor that no one could hold it against him. He had started in the business very young, training the famous Pinder Circus black panther. He sometimes told that episode of his life story—hitting the road at night, the caravans, the big top. He always sounded so nostalgic I wondered how he had ever left the circus and gotten stuck in Vincennes. I imagined him in love with the trapeze artist, her sequined costume sparkling in the spotlights, their secret meetings, the wrath of her animal-tamer fiancé, his sudden departure and voluntary exile behind the gates of the Zoo. The real story, as I would later learn, was quite different.

The head zookeeper started when I took him by the arm, just as he had done. I made him come back and sit with me in the restaurant. I bought him a drink and we sipped in silence. I couldn't help thinking that such run-down shoes must mean he was terribly alone. My own loneliness had never frightened me, but the thought of his suddenly did. What was his life outside work? No wedding band blunted the massive strength of his peasant's hands. The head zookeeper was not a man to be satisfied with ordinary desires—or to inspire them. In a few years, they would make him retire. The employee affairs committee would organize a fine sendoff. The staff would chip in to buy him a ceramic figure of his favorite animal. I had the feeling that despite his ever-present smile and strong, healthy body, he would not survive his release from captivity. He would be found in the kitchen of his small one-bedroom apartment, hanged. I tried not to picture him swinging from his kitchen ceiling like the sides of beef in the Zoo meat locker . . .

I heard the door from the restaurant's front room open and took off my glasses. Jeanne Blin sidled in, clutching her purse to her chest. She stopped near the kitchen to hitch up her stockings, I noticed one of them had a run on the side, from heel to knee. Like a slash from the blade of a sword, the run gaped wider with each step she took, and the way she made her entrance, both embarrassed and smug, brought tears to my eyes.

"Is the meeting already over?" she asked.

The head zookeeper looked into my eyes, and in that instant we became close, if you can speak of closeness between two people whose sole connection is a moment of sadness.

"The Director's not here yet," the head zookeeper explained in his usual kindly manner.

Jeanne Blin feigned surprise. She sat down at our table. I sensed the head zookeeper trembling to think she might figure out she wasn't fooling him, that each and every one of us knew exactly where she had been and why her skirt was rumpled, her hair a mess, and her face smeared with makeup. When the caretaker ordered her a coffee, Jeanne thanked him a bit too heartily, and I saw him turn beet-red. His heart seemed to hang in the wind, swaying with the slightest breeze, the least sign of gratitude. Some evil force took hold of me and made me shatter that private and delicate moment, remarking pointedly on the head keeper's blushing. I was jealous of everyone and everything; I hated myself. I acted the opposite of the way I felt, destroying the atmosphere of trust between us with a few words, as if my rank desires had suddenly spilled on the table, a bitter incontinence of the spirit. The head zookeeper gaped at me, then slowly rose to his feet. The cashier did the same. For a second I thought they were going to strike me. I didn't understand why they were standing there, still and silent. The head zookeeper pointed, and my hands flew to cover my face, like a battered child. I tried to stand up. Firm pressure on my shoulder pushed me back down. I finally realized that my boss was standing directly behind me.

"May I have a word with you, please, Jeanne?"

The head zookeeper pushed his chair against mine to make room for the Director, who unfolded his shooting stick and sat at our table. I tried again to escape, but he wouldn't let me go.

"And you, too, Joseph."

Then he had the astounding gall to accuse Jeanne of leaving her work station half an hour before the posted closing time. He expressed disapproval of her repeated absences, as well as my continual presence in her booth, facts that had been reported to him and that he had personally noted during his daily inspection tour.

"Don't you think something is the matter," he went on, "when a visitor has to interrupt your personal conversations to buy an admission ticket? Jeanne, please, you know what I'm talking about."

Jeanne knew. The head zookeeper's eyes darted pathetically. I put back on my glasses, the real ones, well, the real fake ones.

"And Joseph, was I mistaken to place my trust in you? Your attitude . . . "

Before he could finish his sentence, I retorted that since he could hardly fault my job performance, his criticism seemed unfounded. I have no idea what magic force made me so bold, made the words flow so effortlessly. I pictured the Director pulling out his pocket watch, or fumbling to undo his fly, and somehow I couldn't take his anger seriously. I explained that since the tasks I now performed required only a few hours of my day, I was ready to undertake a project that would fill the time I had been killing at the ticket booth.

"A project?" the Director repeated.

"I would like to take advantage of my trial period to conduct some research on . . . "

I hesitated. The cashier's hand poking through the wooden slats, her lacy bra . . .

"On the integration of *Giraffidae* in a protected environment."

The week before, a student from Maisons-Alfort had been collecting data for a study with that title. None of the other keepers was around, so I was elected to answer his questions. I borrowed freely from him, scrupulously avoiding the word "captivity." The Director was most punctilious about the use of terms designating the concepts of confinement and freedom—and I understand today how right he was. He considered zoo-raised animals to be privileged creatures, freed from the challenges of survival and adapting perfectly to the constraints imposed on them. He maintained that the elephant or the chimpanzee had every chance of living a better life behind bars than left to themselves in a natural setting—provided there was agreement on the definition of "better." However, I steered away from that subject, and the Director greeted my proposal enthusiastically, offering me his help and support, clever enough to understand I was looking for an easy exit, and leaving the path to

Jeanne's booth completely open to him. Encouraged by this new view of things, he shook my hand, and rose to give an impromptu speech citing me as an example to my fellow workers, as he called them, saying I embodied individual initiative and the spirit of enterprise. Then he announced that the staff meeting was rescheduled for the following day. Due to circumstances beyond his control, he said.

# 4

My trial period was extended until winter, then I got a one-year renewable contract, undeniably under-paid, but still affording me a certain credibility with my father. A few weeks after the staff meeting, Jeanne Blin was dethroned from her booth by a smooth-skinned, slant-eyed creature, who removed Jeanne's postcards and tacked up a poster of a pair of tropical hummingbirds fluttering around a basket of flowers. I deeply resented her redecoration and never responded to her daily greetings. The Roman she-wolf disappeared, Norway resurfaced on the lid of a photocopier in the administrative offices. Jeanne had been permanently transferred to the Zoo's accounting department. When I passed by the window to her office, she pretended not to see me. I understood we were no longer on good terms.

Since I had begun to display such interest in the Giraffidae family, and indifference toward the cashier, the Director treated me better than I had ever hoped. I was given unlimited access to the park at all hours of the day and night. The Director himself suggested that I set up some kind of sleep-ing quarters--provided that they would be necessary for my research. I moved a sleeping bag, a lamp, and a few books into the hayloft adjacent to Solange's pen. I was the only employee besides the head caretaker to have a pass key that opened not merely the doors to restricted areas, but also the outer gates. The Director was eager to hear about my work, and so I was obligated to begin noting my observations.

I threw myself into my work so seriously even I was amazed. Within the month, my impromptu project grew to occupy both my time and my mind. I spent hours crouched by Solange, memo pad in hand. The zookeepers were amazed by her docility and my patience--or maybe it was the other way around. The expression on their faces made me feel like they considered both of us freaks. To short-circuit their talk, I decided to put in even longer hours. It wasn't unusual for me to watch Solange half the night. I noticed her sleep was very fragmented. She never dozed more than a few minutes at a time and was highly influenced by the phases of the moon. I reported these pre-liminary findings to the Director. He encouraged me to pursue this avenue of research, which had not to his knowledge been explored, but did not appear to surprise him. When I asked him if Solange's insomnia seemed normal to him, he merely replied that the term was a human invention. He said it with a little smile that implied he knew whereof he spoke.

"Ants," he added, folding up his shooting stick, "never sleep at all."

It was disconcerting to have such tiny creatures compared to my Solange. Still, I continued my nocturnal observations. One fringe benefit was long hours of idle dreaming, my wide-open eyes glued to my protégée's light underbelly. Just where her back legs began there was a fascinating area, a slight swell where the dark spots of her coat gradually faded out, a divinely pure point of departure for my attraction toward Solange.

During the day, to escape the visitors' questions, I would go up to the room where the painting of the Pasha of Egypt's giraffe and her keeper was still hidden. I had studied it long enough to make some sense of the slabs of color blending in the background, a subtle play of thick and thin. As I confirmed a few years later, they represented the territory the man and beast had covered together. First, hovering above them, was a desert zone, deft brushstrokes planting thorny shrubs. This was dissected by a thin line of green branching downward into a blue, dome-studded coastline. As if broken up by the sea, the shore on the other side was lost in spray. Then came a flock of gray clouds, punctuated by the giraffe's red choker, the focal point of the painting. Next was farmland, furrowed with roads, sprinkled with villages of various architectural styles. The springlike look of the woodlands grew gradually darker, ending in a fire of ocher and violet. Just below the inscription, the sun set over a bed of dead leaves, trailing off into nothingness. The bottom five inches of the painting were blank, like Solange's underbelly. What was the painter thinking when he left this empty space? There was not even the slightest clue. Yussef's bare feet appeared against a vacant backdrop. Despite the impression of strength the figure projected, this lack of support gave him a fragile and awkward side. He looked prepared to draw his sword and fight some dangerous if invisible enemy, believing he was defending the giraffe, when it was clearly she who sheltered him from the dangers of this world. Her hoofs stood solidly in the forest; the line of her long neck and her body in three-quarters profile wound gracefully down toward Yussef's head.

But was she really protecting him? The balance of power seemed to shift with the days and my moods. The least little thing could tip it, so that even today I cannot say with any certainty what ties might bind them. There is something snakelike in the way she bends; there is cunning in the man's eyes. What tempting words is he speaking into her ear? What secret thoughts does he try to shake off as he draws his weapon? They are both struggling, against what or whom even the painter doesn't seem to know. Perhaps it is simply the dynamics of finding a way to represent them, forever united, within the restrictions of the frame. The whole thing made me think of those calendars with little cardboard doors you open before Christmas, revealing a new episode of the Nativity story each morning. Sometimes the pattern would vanish, or grow more distinct with just a few quick strokes, like a challenge to the fleeting universe surrounding it. A picture both clear and blurred: there is genius in the combination. Very few images are able to communicate the pleasure of the telling, the process, rather than situation or anecdote.

Despite my research, I have not discovered the painter's identity. There is such a contrast in the treatment of the landscape and the live subjects that I have even wondered whether it might have been a group effort. No single or multiple signature is there to provide an answer. I still think the real creative genius was the man--or woman--who interrupted the artist at work, giving the painting the nostalgic quality of things that remain forever unfinished.

Solange adjusted perfectly to life in the Zoo. Unlike the giraffes born in captivity, she displayed no particular impatience. Only one thing bothered me: I had never heard her utter the slightest sound. The head zookeeper assured me that she was congenitally mute, but I still couldn't believe it. I got him to tell me about lion taming at the Pinder Circus. Armed with that valuable information, I decided I would break the silence separating me from Solange. I was convinced that her vocal organs had not developed in the wild only because she found no one worth communicating with. Her peers might be without vocalization, but Solange? No, it simply didn't make sense.

It quickly became clear to me that I had to establish a coherent language between us. My initial experiments were resounding failures. Despite my efforts, Solange only stared at me in total bewilderment when I tried to get her to make a sound in exchange for food. Bray, whinny, bark, bleat as I might, hoping to stir the memory of some residual voice, Solange remained silent. I waited several months before resolving to use force, but without effect: her only response to pain was a slow blink, and I was exasperated by this silent acceptance of the torture I underhandedly doled out though the bars of her pen. Only the wayward movements of her long neck betrayed her emotions. Whether she was frightened or angry, sulky or satisfied, the grotesque swaying of her neck was the only form of expression Solange seemed willing to entertain. The rigidity of her behavior was unbelievable. How was it possible for such a huge body to have such a limited range of communication? Sometimes I told myself that I was unable to understand her, I was deaf, and that would revive my flagging patience. I made up new games, new experiments. I was learning.

After an entire season of contradictory treatment, I began to have serious doubts about my work--my term for what I later understood was nothing but a long courtship dance. To gather my wits, I would often go up to the artist's loft overlooking the giraffe exhibit. I would picture the Director, a wisp of beard in his teeth; see the woebegone smile on poor Jeanne's face as she rode him like a horse on a whirling carrousel. Then I saw Solange's head, her astonished eyes and long, long lashes beyond the barred window. I spent hours up there, standing motionless by the dust-covered palette, with the dangling paintbrushes for companions. It was a long time before I dared touch the books abandoned in the wooden crate at the back of the studio. There were two or three dozen bound volumes, old texts on mixing colors, but also classic plays and novels. Their presence a few feet from the easel gave them a primordial importance. Could one of them have provided the inspiration for the portrait of Yussef and the Pasha of Egypt's giraffe? I moved the crate into my storeroom and began to read them when I was supposedly observing Solange. As she seemed to take an interest in these objects that suddenly captured all my attention, I got the idea of reading aloud to her, just reading, asking nothing more of her, in the initial phase, than to listen. I thought the sound of my voice might make her try to imitate me, and she might learn to talk in a way. Unfortunately, though I read for hours and hours, no sound escaped from her downy lips. I went from Shakespeare to Dante,

Dante to Dostoyevsky. Sometimes she began to chew her cud right in the middle of some sublime phrase, and I wondered whether Solange really deserved her central place in my life. These revelations of her crudeness threw me into fits of rage, completely disproportionate to reality. It was like having to watch my foster mother pick her teeth with her kitchen knife again. One Sunday, Solange blatantly urinated on a leather-bound copy of Chateaubriands's Mémoires d'outre-tombe that I had left in a corner of her pen. In anger, I stuck her in the rump with the long-handled pitchfork I used to take bales of hay down from the loft. She reared, and from that moment on she accommodated my every whim more obediently than ever. I taught her to turn and to paw the ground on command. The Director was amazed to note how obligingly Solange carried out my orders. "Your trick giraffe," he said after congratulating me, a remark that made my blood run cold.

Solange was trained, of course, but somehow things had gotten off track. I felt that she hated me and that beneath her servility lurked a wild desire to eliminate me. She would have had every reason to, I treated her terribly, but the truth is Solange was all sweetness and light to me. Perhaps deep down I resented her for not resenting me. I often put myself within hoof range to try to provoke the inevitable accident that would leave me half-dead on the floor of her pen. I took unreasonable risks, and still she never tried to get even. The care she took not to step on me when I sat at her feet was incredible, given the narrow confines. She responded to my attacks with an obstinate delicacy. And if her instincts dictated some aggressive reaction, she immediately turned it back on herself.

I was her absolute, uncontested master, and still I doubted. Every single day I needed additional proof, needed to find an original way to brand her as mine. I was possessed by the desire to see her give in to all my whims. I demanded a great deal, and she gave it ten times over. Her generosity exasperated me. Still, I kept reading aloud to her, a practice less useless than it may have appeared. In the end, my persistence paid double dividends: Solange learned to listen to me. I began to enjoy talking to her. Then one night, when she started getting restless in the middle of an excerpt from The Divine Comedy, I hit on the idea of telling her a story of my own. Inspired by the painting of the Pasha of Egypt's giraffe, I described the Nile, the pharaohs, then I related the birth of Jesus, the ox and the donkey bending over the manger, Mary trembling, Joseph searching for some resemblance between himself and the babe.

Solange listened to me, fascinated. The next day, I tried the experiment again. Soon, I completely gave up reading and focused on making up stories. Her powers of concentration grew from week to week. It reminded me of when I used to write to my father, the same pleasure. The main character of these cruel fairy tales was named Yussef. I invented his past, his enemies, his destiny. I even dedicated one of my memo pads to him. I liked imagining him in his native land, somewhere in Africa, saving the young giraffe from the hunters. Words piled on top of each other, I often lost control of what he did. Yussef led me into undiscovered parts of myself, I gave in to his fantasies, trembled with his fears. The farther I went with his story, the more excited Solange got. She rubbed her rump up against the door and hooked her little horns into the handles of her food rack. One night when I was on a particularly good roll, her hoofs began to hammer the ground to the beat of my sentences. Yussef, in this episode, was attacked by a pack of stray dogs on the Marseilles waterfront. He scared them off with his sword, which in the course of my stories had become the mother giraffe's tibia. Solange couldn't take her eyes off me. Just to see what she would do, I suspended my tale in mid-sentence. To my great disappointment, she immediately lost interest in me and began blankly chewing her cud.

How to tell her that I expected more of her, an answer, a question, some sign, at least, of a real dialogue? I called her name and her ears turned toward me. Should I have been satisfied with that mark of recognition? My hero could have been eaten alive by the dogs, it wouldn't have fazed her. I might as well go doze in my loft.

Did Solange sense my discouragement? I was about to turn off the lights in her pen when she finally gave me a sign, kicking hard at the door. The iron echoed through the whole gallery. I heard the giraffes on the other side of the wall start to panic. Then, Solange curled up her lips, and for the first time stuck her black tongue out for me, letting the full length of it hang out of her mouth. I began stroking her with my words again. My hands clutched the bars, it felt like reliving the moment we met, in Marseilles, with me perched on the ladder, poking my head into the dark, and Solange trembling, prancing in her padded crate.

The dogs had quieted and now jumped around Yussef, burying their damp muzzles between his legs. It was especially hot that night.

The next day, the head zookeeper found me asleep in the hall behind the pen. I don't know what lame excuse I made up, I only remember he was kind enough to believe me. He offered to buy me a coffee at one of the restaurant's outdoor tables.

He talked about his childhood, his parents, and I drank in his words. "My father," he said, "was a mailman. All his life he delivered other people's letters but never got any himself. We lived in the Creuse valley, the middle of nowhere, a house in the pines. One morning, just after I turned sixteen, I woke up to the sound of jingling bells: a circus caravan on the road down below. In those days, they still used horse-drawn wagons. I got dressed as fast as I could and ran down the hill to see. A woman was walking alongside the convoy, with a marmoset on her shoulder. She asked me if I knew where they could find some water for the animals, and the monkey hid in her long black hair. I led them to the spring. My father got worried when I didn't come back, and came to find me on his bike.

"This bike," the head zookeeper said, patting his ancient contraption.

"You can guess the rest: that night I helped them set up the bleachers. They asked me to tour with them for the summer. My father gave his blessing. My mother made me promise to write. I guess that's the only promise I ever broke. I learned how to care for the animals, the trainer left, I took over. A few weeks later they brought in the little black panther that made my reputation as a tamer. She had a game leg and no one wanted her: I got to train her. When the man who ran the Pinder Circus saw our number, he made a deal for us both, like slaves."

The head zookeeper sighed. Despite his bitter words, I sensed that he still missed the circus life. I asked how he happened to land at the Vincennes Zoo.

"My panther got sick," he said simply. "The Zoo offered to take her in, and I came with her. I watched over her night and day for quite a few months . . . "

The head zookeeper fell silent. His power-
ful fingers were spread flat on the table in front of
him, as if seeking some comfort in the veins of the
wood. I covered his hands with mine. He pulled
away at once and stood up. I walked him to the
main path with his bike. I liked him.

Once the weather was nice, I was forced to let
Solange out of her private holding pen. I dreaded
the moment when she would confront the outside
world. I had managed to push the date back until
early July, claiming her lungs were too weak, and
no one challenged me. To my credit, I must say that
my care of Solange was efficient and effective. The
veterinarians at the Zoo were full of praise for me.
Sometimes they even came to ask my advice.
Growing up on the farm had given me a very particular, but on the whole very positive, approach to
animal health and diseases. I used prevention more
than treatment, and Solange was never really sick,
except for the controlled illnesses I subjected her to
periodically for scientific purposes. She grew faster
physically than mentally; I treated her like a child,
yet her body was developing at a startling pace.

The day she first went on exhibit, I took up
residence at a sidewalk table outside the restaurant.
That way I could watch her without being bothered
by visitors. I felt like a mother sending her child to
kindergarten. Only the book bag and after-school

snack were missing. Mèrade always used to give me a double ration of chocolate on the first day of school. To my great relief, Solange kept her distance from the herd. She made the other inmates look dull, gray as the concrete and rocks around them. Solange's coat still had the burnished glow of her native Africa. Her hoofs shone in the sun, coated with pitch, black and smooth as little patent-leather shoes. She was adorable.

I let a few weeks go by before I left my command post. Solange got in the habit of keeping me in view. From across the trail I could still sense her skittishness. My ever-present red scarf helped her tell me apart from the other zookeepers. I sincerely wondered whether she would recognize me without it. I didn't dare take it off, preferring to remain in doubt rather than run the risk of confirming my suspicions. Our relationship still seemed too fragile. I waited for summer before swapping my scarf for a beige silk ascot of my father's, sprinkling it with cologne to mask the tobacco smell. The day I wore it, Solange was as glad to see me as ever. From that moment on I felt certain the mysterious kinship between us was not a figment of my imagination. I didn't appear to her merely as a swatch of colors, a scent, a hand that fed, but as someone in three dimensions--plus one: I was Joseph.

Still, to let me know that she didn't appreciate such inopportune changes, Solange sniffed and sniffed at the forage I brought her that morning, shooting me such dirty looks I felt guilty for doubting the depth of her attachment even for one second. Out of pride--at the time, I would have said out of curiosity--I wore my vetiver-scented beige silk ascot for three days straight, and for three days Solange refused to eat anything I touched. She started begging from visitors, a crust of bread here, a peanut there, which she awkwardly scavenged without taking her eyes off me. It was our first contest of wills, and this time I was the one who backed down. I appeared the fourth day with my red scarf on and everything fell back into place. My father, who had been delighted to see me finally surrender this last vestige of maternal influence, simply shrugged his shoulders when I gave him back his ascot. He seemed less and less concerned with life.

Solange didn't hold a grudge. The vet diagnosed a slight case of food poisoning, and she was put on a special diet of soy-milk porridge and cooked onions. She ate it without flinching. We resumed our reading sessions in September. These strange interchanges, which became more emotion-charged by the day, acted on me like a drug. I discovered the feeling of infinite freedom that comes from being not simply listened to, but heard. When I stopped at some point in the story, Solange knew she had to curl back her lips and slide her black tongue out of her mouth. She was irresistible. The character of Yussef took shape in my imagination.

The Director paid my  research little mind now, but still I kept my memo pads. I'd gotten in the habit of jotting down the results of my experiments. I often reread my notes. There was no discernable change in Solange's behavior toward her peers since her arrival at the Zoo: she doggedly ignored them. On the other hand, she often posted herself at the side of the exhibit to watch the ostriches. With almost human concentration, she studied these unfortunate pinched-faced, two-legged creatures. Her curiosity turned into true fascination when an ostrich named Glibett arrived at Vincennes. He was a large, solitary male with missing feathers, acquired from the Tozeur Zoo in a trade involving a pair of gazelles. Accustomed to living alone in a tiny cage, with a soda-loving dromedary and a silent porcupine for neighbors, Glibett found it difficult adjusting to the space he was suddenly offered. Despite the keeper's best efforts, he crouched in one corner, bleary-eyed, scratching the ground. Did Solange fall for him out of pity, or because of her ignorance of the ways of her own species? Did she discover some kinship with this other long-necked, long-lashed animal? If so, she must have had a strange perception of her own anatomical configuration. When she stared down at him, mesmerized by his bald rump, it became painfully clear that the upbringing I had given her could do only so much. I reassured myself with the thought that Solange must have run across some old ostrich during the first few months of her life in Africa, that Glibett was a reminder of her infancy, nothing more. How else to explain the unnatural and totally idealized relationship she and the poor bird established? The head zookeeper told me that in Arabic, the word *Glibett* means sunflower seed, the unshelled snack variety that custodians at my school used to loathe. For such a sizeable beast to be named after a puny seed typified the ridiculous impression Glibett made in spite of himself.

At first their flirtation amused me, but after a while it began to wear on my nerves in a serious way. It was hard to watch my Solange beat a path by the wall between the two pens, deaf to my calls, and unable to answer her suitor's rare lamentations, no matter how much she wanted to. They were only ten feet apart, a paltry distance for animals their size, and therefore even more frustrating. When Glibett moved an inch, Solange followed. You could see the sadness in her eyes if he strayed far from the gate. She imitated him, a pathetic fun-house mirror, nudging the ground with her tender snout whenever he buried his beak in the sand. Glibett's keeper explained to me that during the mating season the female ostrich copied the male's dance to the last detail. How did Solange know that? When the big bird crouched in front of her and displayed his truncated wings, Solange desperately waggled her neck, or her ears, stymied in her search for a body part that might correspond to those twin fans of soft feathers. Then, overcome with excitement, she would turn her back to him, lift her tail high, and urinate.

Solange worried me. Some will say that their show of simple mutual curiosity got me so worked up that I let my imagination run wild, and that my conclusions were based on a highly personal approach to reality, if not outright delirium. Today even I sometimes question the authenticity of my observations, yet my notes back me up: a profound change had occurred in her, undermining our relationship.

To all appearances, there was no cause for alarm. Solange was in perfect health and our reading sessions were not affected by her little fling. She may have snubbed me at times when she was outside, but once I brought her back into her holding pen she was in my power again. I had nothing to complain about, nothing.

Or perhaps everything. The way she went through the usual motions with me, as if Glibett didn't exist, was an insult in itself. The party was over, I got there in time to clean up the confetti. Why was she acting the same? Why did she feel she had to lie? I would have preferred to have her reject me outright, me and my stupid, all-too-human stories. Then I would have been able to make up some new rules. I had any number of ways to pressure her, put a finger in the flooded dike, but first Solange would have to let the cracks show. Instead,

October. Captain Manara cut his price in half, promised to try and keep a steady course; things were off to a good start. The consul crowed from the rooftops that he had crafted an historic encounter, one that people would talk about long after he was gone. Since the fall of the Roman Empire, no giraffe had ever set foot in France. He thought himself quite witty in remarking that it was high time.

Finally the day of departure arrived. Everyone had to get involved. The consul's wife, a yellow-haired Piedmontese, was sure that the cows being sent to produce milk for the giraffe would dry up after a week in the hold. Racked with jealousy, the English consul—one Salt Henry—declared that sea air caused grave cerebral lesions in *Camelidae* and that the giraffe would likely die in horrible pain and, furthermore, compromise the safety of the passengers and crew with acts of un-con-TRO-la-ble madness. He turned the epic into an apocalyptic tale. No one gave a thought to Atir, Yussef, or Hassan the herdsman; yet they were the ones who were to suffer most on the trip.

The ghost of the ostrich often haunted my nights. It took me a long time to figure out that my behavior toward him had been so confused—and violent—because no matter how repulsive he was, Glibett had inspired some very convincing fantasies. At the time I could only climax with the aid of a complex army of images, requiring fresh recruits from time to time. Glibett's war-casualty gait did something to me, strange as that may seem. I imagined him with plumes erect, running full tilt to mount Solange. I got off on making him look ridiculous to her. Often the grotesque vision of the ostrich preening at his Dulcinea's feet, his blunt beak poking into her moist privates, blended with the memory of Jeanne. Where the cashier's stockings ended, her violet-tinged skin bristled unexpectedly with black hairs. The Director accused her of two-timing him with Glibett. He chased her through the Zoo, brandishing his shooting-stick. She was innocent. Solange watched the whole scene with a bewildered look. Finally, she took me in her mouth, her eyes open wide.

I resented Glibett for inspiring such sick fantasies.

All this came back to me a few years later when I was comfortably riding along on a Line 46 bus and a mother with two small children took the seats across from me. I was heading back to the Zoo after a break spent patrolling the platforms at the Gare du Nord. The young woman, engrossed in feeding a tiny thing strapped to her breast, ignored me completely. Far from bothering me, her indifference was thrilling. It was like an invisible screen, protecting me. Behind it I could indulge in my favorite pastime: watching. I huddled in my seat, crossed my arms, and waited. I was fascinated by the nursing infant's determination. It simply stuck its little hand into the dizzying cleavage where it nestled, and a truly awesome breast magically popped out from under multiple layers of shapeless fabric. The baby hiccuped, rooting against the milky skin until it caught the fleshy nipple in its lips. It seemed so much like Solange—a much smaller version, of course—in the way the mouth sought the object of its pleasure, that I was able to overcome my instinctive repulsion and join the baby in savoring the soft and generous warmth of this shamelessly bared bosom. Did the older child guess what I was thinking? She was engrossed, or at least tried to appear engrossed, in tracing something on a foggy window. I could read it clearly against the backdrop of trees and buildings: "NO," she wrote, and the two capital letters were reflected in the cloudy sky. I pretended not to see, but this negative command issuing from her chubby little finger was terribly intimidating. I felt straightjacketed in my emotions, all the more sheepish because my embarrassment must show on my reddening face. Once a teenaged master at the art of concealment, I was now utterly defenseless, undone by the naïveté of this bare-breasted Madonna. She rocked her nursling, oblivious to the world at large. The baby, when it stopped suckling, hung on its mother's dewy glance. Hypnotized by so much sweetness, it dozed off. Then the mother gathered her wits, kissed her little girl, rearranged her gear, buttoned her blouse without even looking. Inevitably the driver would slam on the brakes, wake the cherub, and the whole show started over, without either of them seeming to tire of it. I admired her patience. What I liked best of all was the instant when the baby stirred enough to probe into her blouse and root furiously at the fabric. There was a pathetic energy to it, near-involuntary animal moans came from the tiny throat. If Solange had a voice—and I had resigned myself to the fact she was mute, I had never been able to wring the slightest noise out of her—I thought it might sound something like that.

The bus filled and emptied cyclically. No one attempted to sit next to me. As we passed through the Place Daumesnil, the woman ran her index finger over her offspring's toothless gums, stroking them with the tip of her nail, a gesture so sensual that I couldn't suppress a long sigh of my own. The little girl heard it; still drawing on the window, she gave me a swift kick in the right knee that made me yelp in pain. The mother looked at me reproachfully, as if I might wake the baby, then smiled when I just managed to catch the huge package of diapers teetering on the edge of the seat. Trying to maneuver the baby sideways to change it, she had gotten the straps of her baby carrier tangled, and ended up dumping the infant in my lap before she stood to sort things out. "Do you mind?" she asked simply.

She had a slight foreign accent. Her voice

was calm, very clear.

"He's . . . cute," I mumbled, surprised to see the sweet face the baby was making at me.

"No," she said, adjusting the collar of her blouse, "it's a girl. Her name is Lisa."

What could I say to that? The conversation ended there. I sat still, trembling with fear to think I might make a false move. My pants slowly dampened from contact with the baby. I held her the way you handle a puppy you're trying to sex, with her head against my stomach. Her little pink booties wiggled. The woman stretched out her hands to me. The baby seemed happy to view her mother full-length. The marvelous flow of love between them was contagious; I started to laugh. The baby was laughing too now. The little girl stopped drawing. She stared at me as if I were about to steal her sister, and she had every reason to worry. I pressed the little swaddled body to me and the woman opened her arms. She was leaning over me now, I could see her breasts sway gently. I hugged the baby even closer. An inexpressible happiness attacked me. I squeezed tighter, tighter . . .

Lisa began to wail. All the other passengers turned to stare. My grip eased, the young woman gathered the baby to her with infinite tenderness. She hadn't noticed anything strange and she thanked me. Her trust filled me with joy. She had just given me one of the most beautiful moments of my life.

I often think about Lisa's mother and wish I had gotten off the bus when she did, never let her slip away like that, without a word.  During the bus ride I didn't notice the little girl also had on a kind of harness that went around her waist and over her shoulders; she handed her mother the thin leather reins when they got to their stop.  I helped them pack their things onto a luggage carrier with wheels.  I was steadying it between my legs when I lost hold of the bungee cord and it snapped back at me full force.  The pain was immediate and unbearable.  I doubled over, pretending to tie my shoe.  That was the last they saw of me.

The bus took off and I nearly sprawled into the aisle.  When I glanced out the window, I saw them crossing the square.  They looked like the families of street performers that roam through Paris,  searching for another courtyard where they can display their trick goat or drum-playing bear. The little girl on her leash led the procession, galloping in slow motion like a horse reined in before the start of a race. To my great surprise, the woman limped.  Her gait was too consistently unsteady to be caused by some passing injury.  I thought of the head zookeeper's black panther.  Far from disappointing me, the woman's handicap gave me a glimmer of hope.  We were alike, I could move mountains to try to win her love.  Yes, I loved her, or, more accurately, I could have adored her, the way you adore the memory of a departed soul. At the time, I was convinced I could find her again simply by willing it to happen, and one day or another our paths would cross, by chance, in which I both did and did not believe. At times I tortured myself thinking about her home, her husband, her habits. I felt like killing her for being so far from me, killing her as I took her in my arms, with her baby, both of them naked, squeezing them together until they smothered. Or I would imagine that the four of us lived at my father's, and the little girl was so mean to me that I was forced to strangle her with her own harness reins. I would disguise the crime as an accident. Or else the woman rejected me. She accepted my protection, undressed in front of me, rubbed her swollen breasts while I watched, insisted we sleep in the same bed, but couldn't bear my touch. She got pregnant and tried to convince me that I had had her in my sleep. I begged for details. Her account was overwhelmingly precise. I had to bolt for the bathroom so that I wouldn't ejaculate on her white nightgown, already billowing with a full, taut belly. While I was gone, she went back to sleep. I began to have doubts about myself. I went to a sperm bank to be tested. I masturbated thinking of Glibett's bald rump. I was declared beyond help, unsuited to reproduction. I went for another series of tests, this time concentrating on the image of Solange. My semen was thicker and more plentiful. The nature of one's fantasies obviously had an effect on sperm quality. I felt more confident. A father, I was going to be a father! After an interminable wait, during which I persuaded myself that Lisa's mother was telling the truth, I got the results. I was sterile. I killed her, so she wouldn't be caught in her lie. She didn't suffer; I did. I had to borrow a chain saw from the Zoo to cut her up. I stuffed suitcases full of her into the self-service lockers at the Gare St. Lazare. Mèrade was always a fan of true crime, particularly "trunk murders." When some grisly case was in the news, she would time supper to coincide with the evening broadcast, and we would plant ourselves firmly in our chairs, staring at the radio speaker. A woman's body in seven separate lockers, ten different episodes: with special reports thrown in, it could run six to eight weeks. When the investigation reached a standstill, the perpetrator—eager to stay in the headlines—would start things up again, hastening his own arrest. "Vanity case," he would tip them off from a pay phone, disguising his voice, "Les Aubrais station." A foot, a hand, even better a dreadfully mutilated head would be found. Eventually, the criminal was apprehended. Then cool facts replaced the welter of speculation. A child like me was wildly excited by the methodical process known as reconstructing the crime, as if it were possible to glue the pieces of the victim back together. I dreamed of attending one of these strange festivities. The presence of the murderer, blinded by popping flashbulbs, hounded by every reporter in France, would be the biggest thrill. I would admire his courage, his determination, when he pleaded not guilty on all counts despite the mounting evidence against him. I bought the newspaper every evening and clipped articles for my scrapbook. During recess, when my classmates swapped toy cars or stickers, I dismembered road-kill. I was only interested in cut-up corpses in lockers, other murders left me cold. Mèrade and I thought our predilection for train station trunk murders, which we liked to call railways, set us apart from the common herd of crime buffs. We took pride in detecting a budding tragedy in a few apparently innocuous lines in the newspaper, but our partnership ended there. Once the story unfolded, I identified with the perpetrator, out of habit, while my foster parents sided, in principle, with law and order. The murderers were young, single, gainfully employed; there was no pat explanation for their gruesome crimes. While the murders were the result of long planning, the victims seemed to be chosen at random. By the time I was fourteen, I had catalogued seven similar cases. To my knowledge, railways were not in vogue outside France. Lacking the resources for more extensive research, I gradually lost interest in my bizarre hobby. Instead, I began sending the first alarming letters to my father. The local press had become too limited for me, and my one dream became convincing my father to take me back with him in Paris. Inspired by my daily dose of tabloid journalism, I concocted tearjerkers full of catchy adjectives and shock transitions. I poured on prose so purple my blood vessels popped. Once I slipped up and sent him two accounts of a black eye the same week. He replied very seriously that he hoped my assailants had at least been considerate enough to hit me on the same side. His remark was like peroxide on an open wound. From that day forward I gave up on my railways to dedicate myself body and soul to my new cause. War had been declared. My pen became dry, feverish. I learned how to present him with my inner wounds, inventing them if need be, setting them down with the hint of detachment that transformed humidity into dampness, whiteness into opacity. Nothing interested me besides my suffering. It had always been inside me; now it became full-blown. The substantial increase in the blood money my father sent reinforced the notion that I owed him my unhappiness, it was the only real gift I had to offer him.

There is a demoiselle crane at the Zoo that has spent two years with one of those little cylinders for vitamin C in place of a foot. The makeshift prosthesis blends so well with the stump that it's hard to tell where the bird ends and the metal begins. I often watch her and think about Lisa's mother. In all my rides on Line 46, I have never seen her again. I have made inquiries in the neighborhood around her bus stop, no one knows her. Soon, Lisa will go to school. No doubt her mother will bring her to the Zoo some Sunday afternoon. She'll squeal at the monkeys and suck her thumb. Maybe she'll throw peanuts in their cage. Maybe this time I'll have the courage not to let her get away.

The encounter with Lisa and her mother had some unexpected repercussions. That evening, as I headed back into Solange's pen, it struck me that our relationship was in a rut, a bleak understanding that would never lead anywhere. Our wordless agreement was pleasant enough, but what did I really know about Solange? She slept little, ate what she was given, in moderation; she liked onions, ostriches, the rise and fall of my voice; she steered clear of Beethoven, the male giraffe. Certain details made it obvious she had evolved beyond the primitive creature she would have remained if our paths hadn't crossed, yet many things she did still mystified me. Despite my best efforts, Solange remained impenetrable. Oh, I could indulge in my storytelling, she was all ears, but in fact the adventures of the Pasha of Egypt's giraffe and Yussef the keeper must have bored her. Didn't she keep on chewing her cud during our story hours? Only Glibett had truly excited her since she came to Vincennes, and my brilliant response had been to toss him a poison-soaked pound cake. My petty selfishness and jealousy kept me from seeing that Solange was after more than the big bird's plumeless rump; she was desperate for images from her infancy, the blurred, brightly colored images we carry around inside ourselves. Some old ostrich must have roamed the arid savanna where her mother gave birth to her. Why not admit it? Solange had been weaned too soon, it came to me in a flash as I squeezed Lisa, and the only way to gain her trust was to give her back what she had missed. Yes, we must start over from the beginning, follow in the footsteps of her past, to reach the tender core of her being.

I decided to try bottle-feeding her. The first few times, Solange seemed surprised to see me climb up the double ladder. It bothered her to have me suddenly reach her height. Wasn't her physical superiority her one and only privilege—a privilege of size? As if to show her displeasure, she chomped on the big rubber nipple I'd attached to a bottle, until I was afraid she'd swallow it and choke. However, when I offered her my fingers, she took them delicately in the groove of her tongue and the sucking reflex kicked in quite naturally. It gave me a strange pleasure.

After a few weeks of perilous attempts, I found a way to act as her nursemaid that was safer for me and more natural for her. There was a wooden trap door high on the wall between the hayloft and Solange's pen, designed to deliver her forage directly into the feeding rack ten feet off the ground. The parallel iron bars, solidly attached to the wall, were just at the height of her head, so I learned to climb up to the hayloft, open the hatch, and slip into the feeding rack to give her the bottle. I squeezed the milk into her mouth while keeping my hand on her tongue so she would associate the feel of the liquid with pleasure of suckling. She drank greedily, never hurting me with her teeth. Legs spread, feet dangling, my back to the wall of her pen, comfortably settled on my cushion of hay, I taught Solange to nurse again.

My hunch bore fruit. The bottle swiftly became the center of our mutual concerns. I took great care with its contents. I got permission from the vet to replace part of her daily ration of solid food with a mixture of milk, sour cream, eggs, and bone meal. My purely instinctive choice of ingredients seemed judicious to him. This yellowish mixture was supposed to strengthen Solange's skeletal system, or so I claimed. The slimness of her joints had always baffled me, it amazed me to think such a fragile base could bear so much body weight. When I explained the object of my milk regimen to the Director, he seemed to have reservations, so I invented a new series of experiments to demonstrate the scientific basis of this new tack. I told him it was a question of determining Solange's tastes. Here was my hypothesis: could her appetite and her needs be in direct proportion to each other? Stated in other terms, did she eat for pleasure, or to compensate for some imbalance caused by the conditions of her captivity, and, if so, could this disturbance lead her to eat at the expense of her health?

As I formulated this tangled line of inquiry, I thought of my father. His alcohol intake had increased even more. The Director seemed reassured by the length of my sentences and once again gave me his blessing.

I therefore added natural essences, or various kinds of puréed food, to my formula, and began to note Solange's reactions in a new memo book. Thanks to a methodical exploration, in less than a year I was able to rank the flavors I offered her into four categories: unpalatable, neutral, appealing, and irresistible. The latter included a wide range, from raw onion and acacia, which came as no surprise, to powdered celery and quinine. Furthermore, the mere smell of olives drove her wild. Her tail began to switch, her breathing quickened, little streams of saliva formed at the corners of her mouth, it was impressive. I also noticed her excitement increased in proportion to the salt in the formula. I heightened her natural craving by disabling her salt lick. I had no way of knowing this apparently unremarkable tactic would result in a breakthrough in our relationship. Once I settled in the feeding rack and rolled up my sleeves, Solange would stick out her raspy tongue and, before taking even a taste of her bottle, affectionately lick every square inch of skin I let her have.

I refrained from communicating my conclusions to the Director, and until he retired he was convinced that I was conducting a long-term study—accent on the long—on food preferences of animals in the protected environment at his establishment. "One day," he would tell me, patting me on the shoulder, "one day you'll get the reward you deserve, Joseph, my boy." I spent almost every night with Solange, and he saw that as proof of my extraordinary vocation as a naturalist. He was even rather proud of himself for detecting and nurturing such a strong inclination. He was quite alone in supporting me.

My co-workers disliked me. Except for the head zookeeper, no one could stand my silences. It didn't bother me, their hostile attitude allowed me to behave exactly as I pleased, without any fear of gossip. Since the fiasco with Jeanne Blin, I was wary of supposed kindness from hypocrites. I had made myself a reputation as a loner, and I wanted it respected. If some new employee happened to try and crack my shell—and there are always those charitable souls who want to help bring out the "real you"—I would mutter something inappropriate and put an end to things. If that didn't do the trick, I would raise my voice and utter one or two completely contradictory statements. I had noticed that even people who can take anything you dish out don't last long on a diet of paradoxes.

Often I would begin to cry, for no apparent reason. Fortunately, Solange was there.

One day, I knew why I was crying. I found my father face down on the kitchen table. He wasn't asleep, and he was alone. He was dead. I called an ambulance. They wouldn't even take him to the hospital.

I left my sixth-floor walkup servant's quarters. The lawyer put my father's personal belongings in storage. His share in the apartment building was sold to pay off his debts and cover funeral expenses. I moved to a small hotel in the Porte Dorée neighborhood, close to the Zoo. The owner, thrilled at the prospect of a yearly lease, gave me two adjoining rooms on the top floor, and a bath down the hall. The first thing I did was hammer a nail just across from my bed, where I planned to hang the picture of Yussef. One quiet night I sneaked the canvas out of my secret storage room. I wrapped it up in a big white sheet tied with string. The prostitute on the corner of the Avenue Daumesnil watched me leaving the Zoo as if I were making off with the Mona Lisa. The painting was an unusual format, about two feet wide by almost five feet tall, giraffe-shaped, which must have seemed huge in contrast to my short stature.

Along with my father I lost all worldly ambition.
While before I may have secretly dreamed of making some decisive discovery, after his death my
research reached the level of pointless inquiry, or,
more precisely, research with a point so remote it
remained undefinable. I no longer even felt the
need to set interim goals for myself. As a result, my
relationship with Solange intensified to the point of
banishing anything else. With the passing years, I
kept on bottle-feeding her. I realized that weaning
her again would deprive me not only of a peerless
experience of sharing, but also of a pressure tactic
that was indispensable to her proper upbringing. I
enjoyed her dependence on all the secrets we
shared outside Zoo hours. We had arrived at a ritual that we followed to the letter at every bottle
feeding. It began at the end of the day. I would get
my double ladder and set it up in the middle of the
pen. Solange would go on her own to stand against
the bars and was not supposed to move until I gave
the command. This first step proved to be a difficult
hurdle; the object was to teach her to control her
impulses. It took unsuspected concentration for her
to hold still. She flinched with the least sound, her
ears, jaw, tail seemed to twitch with a life of their
own, beyond her control. However, punishments
and rewards gradually taught her mastery, until her
large, unruly body obeyed her almost perfectly. It
felt like the seal of my mind imprinting the soft wax
of her being when I climbed to the top of the lad-

der, pressed my forehead to her flank, and felt her skin tremble, like the first time.

After months of work I managed to elicit a quiver on command—imperceptible to the naked eye—from this intent and stock-still mass of more than half a ton, and that may have been my crowning accomplishment. No spectacular display ever gave me more pleasure than this subtle proof of my power over Solange. When I sensed she was at her limit, and not a moment before, I would give her the order to move. My voice cracked the silence, sharp and bright as a whip. Solange broke out of her stillness with undisguised joy. I liked to touch the muscles of her calf when she began to prance on the ground of her pen, a spindly-legged young ballerina with toe shoes of horn, her eyes searching the fond crowd of parents. Fortunately, no onlooker could interrupt her awkward and charming dance with vulgar applause. Orphaned, mute, uprooted, Solange had become my privilege, and this was her revenge. I would catch her head and set it swinging front to back like a pendulum. To keep her balance, she would splay her front legs. Coming down from my perch, I steadied myself against her chest, my hands clasping the base of her neck. I dug my nails into her supple hide to adjust the tempo. I wondered how this thick skin, designed to shield her from thorny shrubs in the African bush, could let through sensations of heat and cold, caresses and attacks. It took me years to determine the function and scale of her perceptions with any certainty. The staccato repetition of our swaying threw me into an almost trancelike state of excitement. While I am unsure what impact this ritual had on Solange's slow progress—for after a certain point, we were no longer researcher and subject, but two travelers down the same road—the energy she put into it convinced me that it did something to her, too. Once I had her moving, I would hurry out of the pen. Tearing myself away prematurely from Solange's embrace, I felt I was giving her a taste of the slight bitterness that comes with the best things in life, making them more precious each day, by contrast, by default.

Out in the corridor, doubly protected, I would catch my breath. Solange would stick her muzzle through the bars and watch me back away. She ran through a series of pathetic faces, dilating her nostrils, pouting, batting her eyelashes to beg me not to leave. She did it with such seriousness that I didn't doubt her sincerity for a single instant. And yet, I wonder if her simpering wasn't just more playacting, with Solange as the director.

So I backed out of the pen, to reappear a few minutes later through the trap door in the hayloft, ten feet up. I silently climbed down, slipped my legs through the bars of the feeding rack, and called to Solange. I thought it would occur to her someday to investigate the trap door. But no, she never moved until I softly called her name, and her little horns were always pointed toward the door to the corridor. Her lack of quickness puzzled me. Stupid of me: how could I have believed for an instant that she was really waiting for me at the spot where I'd disappeared? Solange had gained such control over her instincts that instead of running to her bottle, she maintained a theatrical distance. In spite of me, she had worked a twist of humor into our evening ritual; only now I can appreciate its true worth.

The months and seasons flew by. Solange was always able to surprise me; that was her greatest strength. She had reached adulthood with nothing to darken the beautiful mosaic of her coat. When Beethoven got too close, she whacked him so hard with her tail that the message was unequivocal. She didn't even turn around to look at him. She was exquisitely modest. Often I would spend hours sitting at an outdoor restaurant table, just for the pleasure of watching that divine moment when Solange, ears flattened against her head, sent her suitor packing. I could have kissed her, she was adorable. I believed the last phase of our evening ritual was enough to satisfy her animal impulses. I was incontestably the center of her universe. Her fascination with ostriches, to my great relief, had disappeared along with Glibett. In preparation for Lisa's visit, I had taught Solange to bow. When a little girl stopped in front of the exhibit, Solange would sweetly bend her head and paw the ground; it was irresistible. Then she would retreat to the back of the enclosure, awkward and delighted. Sometimes she rolled in the dust or stretched like a cat in the sun. Her shyness enchanted me. Although she observed the rules imposed by the dominant female, Pamela, Solange did not mix with the other giraffes any more than she had the first day she was introduced to the herd. In my opinion, she did not see herself as one of these long-necked, startled-looking animals. It is true that she resembled them only superficially. I mentioned it one day to the head zookeeper, who told me the story of an orphaned peacock in the Vienna Zoo: raised in a terrarium, he never displayed his feathers except to female giant tortoises. Unfortunately, when the multicolored mass of the peacock's tail fanned out, it sent his foster sisters scuttling back into their shells.

I sometimes asked myself if I were acting any differently.

For eight years, Solange staunchly defended her virginity. For eight years, until a certain Friday in April. The Zoo was just opening. Solange, fed and groomed, was standing by the rocks, watching the main entrance. As on every Friday morning, we were expecting the boarding students from St. Catherine's. The Director had given permission for the little girls from this nearby charitable institution to visit his establishment free of charge, provided they did so on weekday mornings, and quietly. We had grown used to seeing them file silently by the cages, clinging one by one to a long black ribbon, like beads on a rosary. Nothing prevented them from letting go of this tie that bound them only in a purely symbolic fashion, yet it was rare to see one of them do so. At the head of the line, the nuns pushed their charges in wheelchairs. It was a while before I grasped the key to their disturbing docility: most of the little girls were blind.

That Friday, Solange seemed even gladder than usual to see the procession appear. She swung her neck up and down, greeting the strange little group in her own way. The amused nuns stopped to watch, and a young woman in civilian dress began a running commentary in a nasal whine. The little girls listened, fascinated by the description of this prehistoric throwback their teacher claimed was bowing down to them. Attracted by the commotion, Beethoven broke off from the herd to try his luck with Solange one more time. He circumspectly poked his head toward her, nostrils dilated, tongue dangling, and then froze. His body seemed to lag behind, ready to desert at the slightest sign of danger. But Solange, engrossed in the sight of her young admirers, ignored him completely. To my utter astonishment, she didn't even move when he began rubbing against her rump. It made me gasp.

The young teacher kept on explaining. "Now the Daddy giraffe is saying hello to us," she asserted. "The Daddy has a big bump in the middle of his forehead."

There was a light ripple of laughter. Then Solange raised her tail high and urinated. With amazing assurance, Beethoven took advantage of her momentary lapse to stick his snout between her legs and take a mouthful of the liquid. He gargled it with lips peeled back, then spit it out in a long stream. The young woman fell silent. A nun studied the clear blue sky.

"It's clouding over," she announced.

Now Beethoven was licking his chops with a dazed expression. I could easily have chased him away, but an unhealthy curiosity prevented me. I wanted to see, yes, finally see. I wanted to be humiliated in the blind eyes of these little girls in uniform. Then Beethoven took up the charge again, bucking, penis protruding like a club. "He's climbing on her back!" exclaimed a redhead with glasses. I could have killed her. The girl next to her went closer to the fence, hands outstretched. The nun roared and the procession slowly got under way again. The schoolgirls, sensing that they were missing something, resisted the pull of the black ribbon. Solange kept swaying, as if none of it concerned her. Deaf to the world around him, Beethoven buried himself in her, engrossed in his guiding spirit, the huge organ sticking out from his groin, as if to give the universe the finger. He penetrated her and she stared at me. A naked look. No sign of pain or pleasure ruffled her cruel, blank stare. I wanted to cry out, but her silence left me speechless. I was dripping with sweat, trembling, impotent. Her doll's eyelashes drooped when Beethoven withdrew.

I spent the rest of the day in my lookout above the ape exhibit. Why hadn't I stopped Beethoven? Why? As if to wipe out the imprint of Solange's stare, I masturbated until I was lost in a thick fog. By the time I went down to feed her, night had fallen. I added a pint of olive oil to her bottle and climbed up into the hayloft. When I raised the wooden hatch into her pen, Solange raised her head toward me, still chewing, and brought her muzzle toward the nipple. Then, for the very first time, I saw her as others did. I noticed the thick skin with cracks around the ears, the greedy lips studded with stiff black hairs, the yellow teeth ringing her gaping mouth, and I backed away, frightened by my own disgust. Solange, my Solange, no longer existed. Nothing was left of her but this awkward mass straining toward me with all its might, a stupid mass  no longer distinguishable from any other giraffe. Yes, Solange was a giraffe. The thought astounded me. The bottle slipped out of my hands. The gooey liquid dripped a few inches from her tongue. Excited by the smell of olive oil, Solange managed to get her head inside the trap door, boosting herself up on the radiator in her pen.

Then the wooden hatch fell back behind her horns, like a cleaver. Sensing she was trapped, Solange struggled to get loose. The injured body writhing against the cement looked like a big lizard, an old chameleon overpowered by too many colors. The hayloft's bare light bulb projected her twisted shadow against the whitewashed walls. I sensed that on the other side of the wall her feet were beginning to give way. Her hoofs banged on the radiator coils as she faltered. I was going to free her, the joke had gone on long enough, I had to go and open the hatch, but some force stronger than myself kept me from doing it. I saw Beethoven's monstrous penis, Solange's eyelids, the clumsy little girls resisting the ribbon that pulled them along. I imagined Solange's belly growing rounder, it was unbearable, her teats swelling with milk, and I left her thrashing, only death could save her now, save her from Beethoven's hold on her, deliver her from herself . . . she panted, eyes bulging, she was strangling, and I backed farther away, I thought about the cashier's hand, her swollen red hand stuck between the blind slats, as if physical love, like death, takes hold of people only to separate them from themselves.

At last Solange grew still. Then from her captive throat came a moan, a quiet, calm little sound. A breath of a voice for the first, the last time, my Solange . . .

For an instant, she was once again the one I

had loved. A sensation of boundless happiness filled me. I had no idea how terribly alone her passing would leave me.

The next morning they found her body hanging full-length, jammed between the wall and the feeding rack, neck broken, eyes rolled back, tongue dangling like a veal head in butcher's shop window. The head zookeeper ran to look for me in the kitchens. I don't know where I found the strength to control my teeming emotions. I followed him up the stairway to the hayloft. The veterinarian was waiting for me. We tore the wooden hatch loose. The body slid in a heap to the floor of the pen. The way her limp neck sagged onto the straw told me that Solange would never deceive me again, that I could be sure of things now. Another journey was about to begin. I felt my legs give way. The head zookeeper's arms shot out to support me. I thought of Lisa's mother, on the bus, and then lost consciousness.

# 6

The ship left the Alexandria harbor to the cheers of the huge crowd gathered to see them off. Everything was fine until the fifth day of the crossing. As he did every morning, Yussef went to feed the giraffe personally—he was the only one who could handle her, without him she would have starved. Hassan had delivered the two pails of warm milk to the foot of the mizzen mast. Sensing that her breakfast was on the way, the giraffe pranced in the hold but stayed cool on the bridge. As promised, Captain Manara had rigged a straw-lined tarpaulin so her head could poke out into the fresh air. She appeared to suffer no ill effects from this semi-captivity. The way she danced from side to side was the only outward sign of her impatience. Since the captain had ordered one of his sailors whipped for addressing her inappropriately, the crew had kept its distance. A sheet of oilcloth stretched over four stakes protected her from the sun, the rain, and the birds' offerings. Yussef spent the better part of his time huddled beneath this shelter, his back ramrod straight against the giraffe's neck. His whole spine felt her breathe. Thus he managed to forget that around him there was nothing but water, salt water, and more water *ad infinitum*. Then another, no less agonizing, vision came to him: it wasn't the sea holding up the ship, but the ship holding back the sea. And the earth was only a crumbling pot made of clay, a nicked and hollow marble . . . Around the giraffe was the bridge, around the bridge, the hull; each piece of the brigantine, and soon the entire universe, appeared as a series of rings widening out from the animal's neck. There he was, Yussef, leaning against the master beam of the world, with only a sun-bleached tibia and worn sandals for weapons. He found no glory in it, quite the contrary. He could topple the whole structure in the blink of an eye and they would all disappear, smothered. Fortunately, the brick-red ribbon around the giraffe's neck held a silver locket with a verse from the Koran inside it, giving her a sovereign power. When Yussef was about to dream his way over the edge, he would grope for the amulet, eyes riveted to the horizon, and grip it with all his might like an infant clinging to its mother's breast.

This is what happened—or should have happened—that morning of the fifth day. The young giraffe was quietly drinking her milk when Yussef noticed the necklace had disappeared. He leaped up, searched the straw, went shrieking below decks, resurfaced . . . nothing. A sailor ran to tell Hassan that his companion was behaving strangely. The herdsman hurried up to the bridge, just in time to spy Yussef swinging the bone over his head in pursuit of a groggy Atir, who staggered toward the bow, still in his nightshirt. They collided by the lifeboat and lit into each other with a vengeance. Hassan tried to pull them apart, but the tibia smacked him in the face and knocked him out before he knew what had hap-

ng means: total surrender to the whims of the
who loves you. Passing into legend, Solange
granting me one last privilege—being able to
sess her as I never had in her lifetime.

So every Friday for three straight years I went
commune with Solange's remains. I paid dis-
t homage to the seven vertebrae of her neck.
ng them strung on a metal rod, I wondered how
had ever worked in her lifetime. All the other
fes on display in the gallery were stuffed, leav-
olange in solitary splendor, freed from her yoke
sh, immense and delicate. I invented ways to
myself feel I was indispensable to her. For
nce, I told myself that I absolutely must keep
ye sockets clean. It was terrible to see my
ge with dust in her eyes. I even bought a
r duster with an extension handle especially
e job; I still have it in my room, the gaudiest
you can imagine, hot pink and green. It
me think of the Vienna Zoo's orphaned pea-
I thought about dyeing the feathers black so
y dusting wouldn't attract the guards' atten-
ut then gave up on the idea. Even immacu-
dusted, Solange's eyes would still be blind.
took it into my head to swipe one of her
and bury it in the square behind Notre Dame.
didn't have the heart to rob her skeleton of
so essential to its balance, the tibia would
be replaced with a newly cast imitation. I
o be replaced with a newly cast imitation. I
dare go through a sculptor, although that

pened. Atir would not unclench his fist until Captain
Manara arrived on the scene. The sacred talisman rolled
to the gunnel. It was open. On a piece of parchment
folded like a fan was a verse from the Koran: *Do not
walk proudly on the earth. You cannot cleave the earth,
nor can you rival the mountains in stature.*

The red ribbon was never recovered. Hassan
escaped with a bandaged forehead he hid beneath his
headdress. Atir couldn't bear the giraffe now. As if to
get even, the giraffe would open her mouth, peel back
her lips, and dangle her long black tongue every time he
approached. She would freeze in this bizarre pose.
Some days, she almost seemed to squint. A stream of
drool formed between her lips. Neck lolling, blank-eyed,
she waited. No, Atir could not bear her.

*I due fratelli* dropped anchor in Marseilles on 26 October
1826, after seventeen days at sea. The Count of
Villeneuve-Bargemont, Prefect of the Bouches-du-
Rhône, welcomed his honored guest as discreetly as possible. The giraffe favored him with a most indulgent
look.

The weeks that followed Solange's passing remain
stamped on my memory as the darkest period of my
life. The Director ordered me to take some vacation
time: I apparently frightened children when I
walked the park trails. Did he want to shelter me

from the investigation, if there ever was any investigation? I spent an entire month in my hotel, staring at the painting, racked with guilt. I expected the police to come and deliver me from this slow torture, but no one came, no one.

When I went back to work, I sensed that my colleagues had been asked to be nice to me. I started wearing my thick glasses again. They would lower their voices and mention the "terrible accident," or say "What a mistake, that radiator by the feeding rack, and the trap door . . ." They blamed Solange's pen, never suspecting any involvement on my part. Every night before he went home, the head zookeeper would ask me to have a drink with him, and that was the only thing keeping me at the Zoo. He told me stories, I listened to him silently, like a child. He grew passionate describing the first wharf rat landing in the Volga delta, Astrakhan, 1727, then spreading through the Orient. "The rat and the mosquito love humans," he concluded, "it can't be helped." I constantly longed to cover his hands with mine, as I had once before, but I didn't dare. One day, he announced that my protégée's skeleton was to be put on display at the Museum of Natural History, and I couldn't keep from touching him. He did not push my hands away.

Strange as it may seem, this news lifted a great weight off my shoulders. Having Solange acknowledged by Science made me feel even surer she was immortal, and so were the ties that bound

us. Having her body materialize some[...] me to gain a certain distance. Re[...] exhausting emotion, but bearable wh[...] fingers can grasp a clearly defined o[...] soon as Solange was put on exhibit, [...] my week with long sessions of ator[...] Museum. Like the days when I use[...] vast lobby of Gare St. Lazare, I so[...] mind roaming beneath the main gall[...] ing. I even went as far as to sign up [...] ture series so that the guards wou[...] wonder why I was so infatuated with[...] bones holding no particular fascinat[...] eral public, their considerable size n[...] One detail, however, might have c[...] tors' imagination and distinguish[...] from the bulk of ordinary remains[...] her feet gave her date of birth as or[...] on the Cape of Good Hope, whic[...] pure fantasy. I could easily have[...] truth, but what was the point? S[...] like an old maid lost in her mem[...] on Christmas, at the meeting poi[...] under the radiant sun of a sadly [...] to end your days caged behind [...] Joseph as a keeper—it was food [...] far from displeased that the Mus[...] grace her with mythical origins. [...] by, I would remain the only or[...] the true facts of her odyssey. P[...]

would be best. I had read that the new resins they
used dried in a matter of minutes. To make my task
easier, I asked the Director to help get me work at
the Museum during my yearly August vacation. I
don't know whether he tried. He was very preoccupied at the time, getting ready to step down. For
several years he had been pushing his retirement
back from one season to the next. No one really
believed he would go. At any rate, on one of my
Friday visits that spring I found the doors to
Solange's gallery closed to the public. The guard
explained that the roof was leaking on the kanga-
roos, the wiring was faulty, and the hundreds of gallons of alcohol in the specimen jars made the place
a virtual powder keg.

So my long vigil over Solange's earthly
remains ended, without a sign of farewell. I often
think of her body, straight and tall among the stuffed
and mounted hippopotami and whale skeletons in
that immense iron-and-glass sepulcher. The renovation was apparently postponed due to lack of
funds. A construction project involving a huge
underground storage vault for the sleeping animals
captured the administration's attention. Everyone is
waiting, and Solange's eyes are piling up with dust.
To console myself, I often walk the Museum
grounds. I sit on a bench in the shade and watch
little girls and their mothers go by. When the park
closes, I run back to the safety of Vincennes.

Since Solange's death, I have been assigned to

care for the giraffes in general. It feels like a giant step backward, to when I was a gawky teenager blushing behind the Director's goldfish tank. I'm bored. I barely recognize myself at times, I feel like such a failure. Condemned to loneliness, I creep along, my sickening past hanging over me like a threat. Nothing interests me, everything perturbs me. I'm no more than a mishmash of undigested memories, a can of something past its expiration date, swelling with stale, fermenting thoughts. I ask myself too many questions, that is the problem. Or rather, my job leaves me too much time to think. I know it does, it's just another item on my list of useless torments. I miss Solange. With her, nothing I did, nothing I thought was without a purpose. What insane impulse made me turn her into a long procession of bones? Fourteen ribs, including seven false ones; forty-three vertebrae, with only seven in the neck. She was my mother, my child, all I had found again, all I lost. Solange, my darling, come press your lips to my forehead, come back to be with your Joseph. Can you understand that I've changed?

Life is slowly leaching out of the Zoo as well. In two days they are throwing a party for the head zookeeper's sixty-fifth birthday. I can't get used to the idea that he will have to retire. He never talks about it. What will become of me? The Director finally did leave, then Jeanne Blin, and droves of others. For the last six months, the new management has been pushing through a major restructuring. The talk is all streamlining, profitability, quality. They say business is already better. The number of female trainees is down by half. They don't dare ask me to leave, but I know they'll jump at the first excuse to lay me off. Until then, I'm staying on, performing flawlessly (for what it's worth), going in circles in this overlarge enclosure. I walk. To kill time, I have created a code of behavior, with its own strict limits, logic, priorities. No light can penetrate to the dense core of this robot-like existence. There are certain parameters that must be very closely followed. I avoid the administrative offices and spend long hours observing the vultures near what was once Jeanne's ticket booth. A ruff of feathers seems to divide their bare necks from their bodies. They bring back my old nightmares. I am both amazed and disturbed by the fascination I feel for things that used to terrify me. Every day I go up to my old salt storeroom above the ape exhibit. I always ejaculate in the same spot, like a dog marking its territory. Cold comfort in these sticky drops that leave a whitish film on the asphalt when they dry. I collect the remains of my transgressions in a little box, with a brush, and bury them each month near the giraffe exhibit. Any variation in my daily routine, no matter how infinitesimal, can disturb my sleep for weeks. The worst disgrace always comes from breaking a law you have made yourself. I feel myself becoming my own master, my own slave. I give myself orders. I obey myself. It feels good to be both the tamer and the animal. I dread the fast-approaching day when my self-imposed constraints no longer supply me with the inner freedom I crave. So I walk, snug in my brick-red scarf, trying not to forget for one moment. My mattress is still in the hayloft. I spend most of my nights there. When I hear the first sounds from the animals at daybreak, I even feel happy. Once the Zoo opens, I turn back into the surly attendant I have always been, answering grownups' questions with a few curt words, if at all. Now that Solange is dead, the only conversations I enjoy are with children. They are a bit like her, open and disarmed, ready to believe, to share anything. My favorite thing is to take them behind the boulders, show them the mysterious world hidden from the public. They shriek when they see the rows and rows of sides of beef in the basement locker, and I feel less dejected. I want them to remember it all their lives, so that long after I am gone they still talk about their behind-the-scenes tour of the Zoo. The parents are on their guard—do they think I don't notice?—and beam nervously at their offspring. They needn't worry. I know now it is wrong to imprison your dreams, or you might end up all alone looking at the skeleton of your lost love. A firefly's light is snuffed the moment you touch it. When I approach these little girls in pig-tails, even the idea of desire evaporates. I am satisfied to look, hoard impressions, imagine.

Why do I always have to trick myself into experiencing the least pleasure? My existence is a slow whirlwind of images that both oppress and protect me . . . I often fixate on abstract things, the sharp contrast of two colors, the neck of a vase, the shape of a package, the sway of a crane. It is rare for human beings to play any direct part in my fantasies. They are used only as objects, fragmented, unaware, interchangeable. The notions of attraction and repulsion are foreign to me, or too closely linked, probably, for me to fathom. I like the surprise of an unexpected glimpse of skin, a snail slowly creeping along white tile, the bustle of passengers in the Gare St. Lazare. I like pissing in the street at night (watching sidelong for passersby), exciting the elephants from a distance, and walking, walking . . . I like many things, come to think of it, yet the idea of having a woman beside me in a bed is no more appealing than ever. I think nudity would bore me. Coming is a painful ordeal, a danger, you go outside yourself, forget yourself. Perhaps it's a question of training, I don't know. I feel like it's too late for me. Watching the men who prowl around the Zoo is certainly no inspiration. They are still so strongly conditioned to reproduce that they feel overwhelming guilt unless their pleasure involves some semblance of copulation. Hard-up males go looking for a female in the woods and pay her, it's painfully clear. I'm glad I'm not like them.  Simply observing the world around us reveals far less vulgar ways to seek thrills, or satisfy one's needs, as some people might put it.  Since Solange's passing, for instance, I am strongly drawn to public transportation.  Perhaps I use the bus so often secretly hoping to run into Lisa.  The subway has its charms as well, especially at rush hour.  I feel a more tightly condensed version of the strange convergence of space and beings that struck me so profoundly that first time up in the storeroom, watching the apes.  In the subway, enclosed and in motion, riders instinctively find their places, so gracefully there is a hint of genius in it.  Their ability to ignore one another enchants me.  In the middle of the front car, a little boy twirls around the post.  In each of the four corners, men are sitting on the fold-down seats.  An old woman is lost in her knitting.  She's dead, yes, for a second I believe she's dead.  The stops speed by, the directions are clear, each person goes his own way.  The image of this long, articulated caterpillar burrowing under-ground is in itself a deeply disturbing thought.  I think of the complex network of all these lives, thrown together for the length of a subway ride, crammed tight and avoiding contact, locked in, at one another's mercy, and I come.  How to explain it?  Only Solange could have understood me.

Keeping one's distance is the hardest—and most exciting—card to play in these promiscuous circumstances.  I admit giving in two or three times to the temptation to rub up against someone, but this garden-variety fondling never took me beyond the stage of a halfhearted erection. However, exposing myself to potential rejection and humiliation is a crucial part of my erotic repertoire. I like the thought of being seen by a third party, being seen seeing. Partners in crime. I have never gone far enough to provoke an attack in public. I stay just outside the limit, flirting with danger, skirting catastrophe. In this perilous state, I still manage to find some pleasure.

I dream of being everywhere at once, inside and out, actor and spectator. Equipment can be a versatile aid, as I first learned from an anonymous work in the Bibliothèque Nationale entitled *Correspondence*—the title caught my eye when I was searching for a possible published version of the letters I had sent to my father. It was the story of a most bizarre crime wave. A police court verdict dated 1 February 1820, sentenced one Auguste-Marie Brizeul, profession apprentice tailor, to five years in prison for having *pricked* one Miss Victorine Pommier from behind with a stiletto-tipped cane. According to information from police headquarters, at least sixty similar incidents had been perpetrated in Paris in less than three years. The prickers operated in the evening, when the Opera let out, or around the theaters on the Grands Boulevards, attacking only very young women.

These few lines made a strong impression on

me. For one man arrested and tried, how many more must have tested their skill undetected, and how many more had dreamed of doing the same?

I got the idea of buying an umbrella last winter. No one of those folding affairs you stick in a bag, no, a real black umbrella with a wide, curved handle that easily grasps fabric. I spent hours perfecting my technique, practicing on an old overcoat hung in the middle of my hotel room, before venturing down into the subway. I had quickly rejected the idea of the stiletto; the whole point was to use an accessory as an extension of the body. It seemed to me I would attain sensations even more heightened because they were indirectly stimulated. I trembled the first time I darted beneath the pleated skirt of a young woman with her back to me. She didn't move. The train was packed. Every time it braked, I felt the wood pivot slightly against her tights. After three stops, she stepped aside, supposedly to let someone get out. I was in such a state that this simple shift in position made me ejaculate. I moaned softly. The young woman, thinking she had bumped into me, excused herself. I was embarrassed for her.

With experience, I learned not only to control myself, but also to choose my partners more wisely. Loose dresses and roomy coats, if less revealing than short, tight clothing, offer innumerable possibilities. I have seen heavily-clothed legs instinctively place themselves within the reach of the handle and initiate the back-and-forth movement on their own. Masculine clothing is, unfortunately, less suited to this sort of operation. Jackets are too long, trousers too thick. And while men may be willing to play along, they ignore the basic rules: keeping your distance and proceeding in strictest secrecy. As in other areas of life, men display their thirst for possession. They need to consummate, engulf, penetrate. Or else they grow oddly shy, turn off to any tactic. Teenaged boys may look like easy targets, but it never works with them. Trapped in their unruly bodies, they blush and push away, afraid even to show their confusion.

Once, when I used to haunt the train stations, it happened to me. I was approached by a pervert, as I would have said at the time. I must have been sixteen or seventeen. The memory of it terrifies me still.

# 7

Now that the giraffe had taken up winter quarters in the Marseilles City Hall, everyone flocked to the prefect's receptions, no longer turning up their noses at the Count of Villeneuve-Bargemont's invitations. The whole town talked of nothing but the king's new animal. The prefect's wife was overjoyed. "Just look at that tongue," she gloated, clucking with pleasure at the sight of her charge, "it looks like, like . . . "

Plucking a handkerchief from her ample bosom, she stifled a burst of laughter unsuitable to her station in life. "Like a big black worm," she finally blurted, overcome with excitement.

The guests elbowed each other. The count resumed his explanation: "Had to move heaven and earth to get her out of quarantine before the date stipulated in the health code. We learned the hard way that there is such a thing as an honest official."

His tone of voice betrayed the fact that he was not entirely indifferent to his wife's remarks.

"She uses that thing like a hand," the countess whispered in her neighbor's ear, "you absolutely must come some morning to see how she licks her Negro's face, it's a touching sight."

She pronounced it "knee-grow," with an aspirated N.

"And those little horns," the baroness chimed in, "aren't they adorable?"

"Adorable, indeed," grumbled the baron.

The prefect's wife made sure no one left without exclaiming over the length of her distinguished guest's eyelashes. One evening, the intrigued young giraffe approached its admirers. They retreated in a silken rustle.

"There," exclaimed the countess, "she's sticking it out, look, look!"

The wine had flowed freely at dinner. The smell became oppressive. Someone suggested the coffee must be getting cold in the drawing room.

Soon it was all over town that the countess had taken a fancy to one of the Sudanese attendants. The gatekeeper had spied her crossing the courtyard in her nightclothes at three in the morning. She claimed to have misplaced her lorgnette. The chambermaid squirreled away a piece of straw she found on the floor of the master bedroom. And yet Their Excellencies were on the best of terms. Was he blind? Was she sleepwalking? The local bourgeoisie made the most of the rumor. The heartsick countess had to leave town to quash the gossip. The count organized a "Giraffe Night" for local businessmen and bureaucrats. The following week, the medical and legal professions were graciously invited. Then the common people's fury was aroused; why should they be excluded? Night and day, mounted police had to

It took me a few seconds to react. When he raised his index finger and held it in front of his mouth, imposing silence on himself, I noticed his fingers were deeply stained with nicotine. I motioned that no, I didn't want any breath mints. He frowned and shook two tiny, dark rectangles into the palm of his hand, then popped them into his mouth. "Down the hatch," he said, undaunted. I smiled at him, despite my eagerness to get back to my work. Next he offered to help me, in an extremely roundabout way, saying he was sure to learn something in the process. I protested, but since he insisted loudly and the other patrons were beginning to stir, I wrote the code on a slip of paper, pointing to the letters X, Y, and Z on the other side of the cabinets. "That's all?" he snickered, and went to get a form, filling it out right under my nose with his name—Colin B.—the code, and the number of his seat in the reading room. Then he sauntered off toward the main desk.

I was still hard at work, resolving not to allow any more distractions, when he came back with the triumphant announcement that my request had been entered, despite its fragmentary nature, but the volume in question would not be available until after lunch, since shelf searches were suspended between noon and two. He motioned toward the librarian with a wink. "An old acquaintance," he said, as if to explain himself. I thanked him.

"Expect the worst if you want to have the

best," he murmured in my ear, pulling me toward the stairway, "things move so slowly here . . . But everything is shelved numerically, no need to know the author's name! Clerks on roller skates, miles of stacks, shelves as far as the eye can see. Very logical. Old-fashioned, granted, but efficient. And lunch is on me, of course, don't even try to argue."

Disjointed as his remarks were, I followed him, afraid my research would suffer if I refused. The moment we were outside the building, he lit a cigarette. As he inhaled the smoke, his phrases grew lengthier. He led the way into a Tunisian restaurant. The staff seemed to know him. He ordered a salad for himself, selling me on the house special couscous; I'd eat it down to the last bite, he promised. He talked a lot, rushing, mumbling. Fortunately, our food arrived promptly. He watched me eat as if each mouthful were the most sensual of promises. What he told me was not without interest. He expressed himself elliptically, playing leapfrog with his sentences, which made the conversation difficult—and intriguing. He reminded me of a teacher I had in tenth grade, one all the kids ridiculed, who attracted me in a way. His approach to teaching math was passionate and subtle. That year we had geometry, and I remember lavishing attention on the homework for his class, deliberately neglecting my other subjects, hoping he would decipher the signs of my attachment. Over dessert, I learned that the breath-mint man had also taught high school, in a Paris suburb. I could just imagine how his students must have treated him. He explained that he was taking a year's leave of absence to complete a study of kinship in desert sheepherding communities, and spent his time shuttling between libraries. He had never done any field work, he told me in his scattered fashion, for fear of being disappointed by reality. His method consisted of encircling the subject in the most indirect fashion, then slowly coming closer, so as not to frighten it, until it was trapped in a tight web of knowledge. His arm traced a wide spiral. He was still some distance from the central point, and seemed in no hurry to get there. We were both fascinated by the same things, the pleasure of circuitous routes, outskirts, connections. In a few luminous (and complete) sentences, he formulated a defense of the word lucubration, "in the original sense of the term, meaning to burn the midnight oil, from the Latin *lucubrare*, derived from *lucere*, 'to shine.' " Lowering his voice, as though making a guilty admission, he told me he sometimes went for days without sleeping, convinced that lack of sleep and scholarly toil would combine to bring him an epiphany. With these words, he pulled a little blue medallion of the Virgin Mary out of his pocket and kissed it. I thought of the holy card stuck behind the painting of the Pasha of Egypt's giraffe. A pile of cigarette butts grew in one corner of the platter of loukoum. I recognized the metallic whiff of meals during my late teens, when my father, intimidated by my relentless silence, hid behind a smoke screen of black tobacco. Only his serial sneezes managed to rouse me from my torpor, awful explosions that sent ashes flying and me to dump the contents of my plate in the garbage and go lock myself in my servant's quarters.

Colin B. rattled on and on. "Men have to realize," he was saying now, "the difference between the necessary and necessity. The body, the soul. Masculine element, possession; feminine, ineluctable constraint of the spirit. I hate shortcuts, it's a fact, I prefer the long way around . . . "

After that I lost track of his chatter. He didn't seem to care whether I understood. My glass kept filling up with Tunisian blush, I drained it without thinking, and when I got back to the hushed, anonymous atmosphere of the library, what I wanted most was to go to sleep. Colin B. walked me back, gathered up his things, and left me his seat. Without even saying goodbye, he hurried toward the door. The clock read 1:35 p.m.; I still had twenty-five minutes before my request would be filled.

From my seat, I could see the trees, the rosy glints of the botanical gardens' greenhouses. The memory of Solange banished the image of Colin B. I felt sleep wash over me. Only a few hundred yards away, her skeleton watched and waited. Poor

Solange, alone in the midst of so many stuffed and mounted mammals, her eye sockets thick with dust. Today, it was my turn to suffer for her. But how, to what ordeals should I subject myself? Wasn't her absence punishment enough? Two weeks before Solange's gallery closed for good, I went into one of those white trailers you see on the outskirts of Paris. For a fifty-franc note, they read your fortune. The curtains were drawn, only a small lamp with glass pendants illuminated a crystal ball and two decks of ordinary-looking playing cards. I was about to leave when a grave voice asked me to please be seated. I jumped. "The thing," I heard it whisper. "There is someone with an object in a hand. Cut!"

A round, bearded face appeared at the back of the tiny room. His made-up mouth stretched into the semblance of a reassuring smile. "Cut!" he repeated.

An object, a hand . . . Cut what? I paid and went back out in the street without understanding what was happening to me. I ran straight ahead, as if to shake off some terrifying hallucination. An object, a hand . . . A hand cutting the metal links, the seven vertebrae of Solange's neck detached and scattered on the hard stone floor. A slender paint-brush dipped in a bottle of India ink marking an indelible brand on each of her bones, one after the other. Solange as a box of spare parts stacked in a cabinet. Solange scattered behind the showcases in the comparative anatomy lab. Reassembled in a museum in La Rochelle, Lille, or Verdun, next to an old stuffed ostrich. Fondled by a pimply underling, measured, classified, forgotten. And I, her creator, her master, chasing down any lead for a fleeting glimpse of this dismembered body. An object, a hand. Cut! Closeup of her skull, studded with precious stones, a treasure venerated by some obscure sect. Aerial shot, the tracks of her final sprint across a thorny valley east of Transvaal, the last traces of her free existence. The secret of her determination to remain faithful to me, her devotion, a jigsaw puzzle of bones for sleepy, conscientious scientists to pore over. Oh my sweetheart, my Solange, without you I am nothing, I miss you, I long to feel the touch of your lips on my skin, I miss you . . .

"Mr. Colin," I heard someone say in my ear, very loud, "Mr. B. Colin." I had slumped like a schoolboy at his desk, head on my folded arms. A woman waved an index card under my nose, explaining that document requests were filled at the table next to the central desk, right near the front door. It was up to the individual reader (she stressed) to pick them up. It was almost 5:00 p.m.; I had slept more than three hours, a tiring sleep, heavy with jumbled dreams, too close to reality not to trouble the mind long after waking. I stood and walked unsteadily to the designated table. Under a wooden paperweight I found a brochure published by the Friends of the Museum of Natural History. On a strip of paper pasted near the top of the gray-green cover was a code number matching the one I copied off the holy card. Only then was I fully awake.

The publication opened with the minutes of an association board meeting. My hands trembled turning the pages. I reviewed each line, searched every listing for some clue to the relationship between this musty document and the painting from the Vincennes Zoo. From Reverend Father Teilhard de Chardin's Mongolian expedition to the reorganization of the arachnid collection, I found nothing even remotely connected with the picture. I came apprehensively to the final article. Then, from the very first words, my patience was rewarded.

The author, named Biers, related the journey of a giraffe, the Pasha of Egypt's gift to King Charles X, crossing France on foot early in the last century. Excerpts from the letters of Geoffroy Saint-Hilaire, professor of Zoology, founder of the menagerie at the Jardin des Plantes, to the Count of Villeneuve-Bargemont, Prefect of the Bouches-du-Rhône, rounded out the narrative. The first dispatch, dated 21 May 1827 and sent from Aix-en-Provence, ended like this:

*Our progress could hardly be better. Everyone knows what he must do, and does it. By that I mean man and beast. Your friend Atir, proud as a peacock to be in charge of a bridle rein, has*

*gained the respect of the Marseilles grooms. As
planned, the right harness rein position has fallen to
the young Negro Yussef. Since we left Marseilles, I
have not once seen him leave his charge's side. His
devotion is limitless. As for Hassan, he is driving
the cattle. His Honor the Sub-Prefect of Aix must
have reported to you on the crowd's excitement at
the sight of the giraffe. Their shouts rose like a single cry, though a long and exceptionally loud one.
There was widespread admiration for this animal
towering above anything human, majestically swaying its head in the breeze and grazing in the tree-
tops. And this is no more a matter of chance than
anything here below.*

I pulled my memo book out of my pocket, and
without even reading the rest of the pamphlet,
feverishly began copying the passages concerning
the giraffe and its keepers. My eyes brimmed with
tears. Here it was in black and white, printed in
Vesoul in 1923, catalogued in the Museum Library.
I wasn't dreaming. The farther I went in the text, the
more I seemed to move beyond anecdote or coincidence and into that evanescent realm Colin B.
would have called fate, which I would define as a
certain fluid state transcending mortal man's usual
notions of time and space. Between these lines I
traced my footprints from Marseilles to Paris, and
the final proof (as if the painting from the Vincennes
Zoo weren't proof enough) that a century and a half
earlier Solange had already laid her terrible, sweet

eyes on me, her abandoned child's eyes. I felt her warm breath on my cheek. I saw myself crouching in her pen, reinventing the character of Yussef for her. Images fell into place with imperturbable logic: the painter winding a stroke of red around his giraffe's neck, my mother knitting her scarf, Solange sticking her head through the trap door in the hayloft and the wooden slat falling back behind her ears, Malcolm leaving fang marks on my skin . . .

At this memory, I shuddered. I was suddenly afraid, afraid of the signs that pursued me, the weight of my name, this double heritage too heavy for a child of thirty-three. I dreaded the moment when I would have to turn in the pamphlet. A strange sense of privacy made me wince at the thought of the research librarian poking her weasely eyes into it.

A bell signaling the closing of the library broke my train of thought. My pencil kept flying over the notebook.

*Paris, 12 July 1827. Your Excellency,* I copied, *I have finally brought my mission to completion. Last Monday, the giraffe was presented to the king. I was still suffering from urinary retention and inflammation of the urethra. I dragged myself to St. Cloud and consulted my aches and pains to see if I should proceed or retreat. I appeared at court and was able to discharge the burden of this audience, which had fallen entirely on my shoulders.*

I stopped for a few seconds and looked

around. The other readers seemed in a hurry to leave. Poor Geoffroy Saint-Hilaire! With his urinary retention and urethritis, he seemed so much like my Director that I could only picture him with a shooting-stick and the formidable freedom of mind old scientists are supposed to have. I contemplated a modern counterpart for the stableman Atir. I thought of Glibett, the envious rival, the other man, prepared to stoop to anything to keep his place at the head of the procession. The letter ended with these words:

*His Majesty wanted details about the giraffe's grooms. I called his attention to Yussef, Atir, and Hassan. He sent for the Minister of the Interior and ordered him to allow them each 2,000 francs, which was carried out, to the men's great satisfaction.*

*The countess will be relieved to hear that while Atir and Hassan have decided to return to their native land, Yussef has agreed to stay with our adoptive daughter until her permanent removal to the Jardin des Plantes.*

The bell rang for a second time. Outside, it was raining. I didn't have my umbrella. My neighbors were packing up their pens and notes and congregating around the central desk. I stayed in my seat, with my back to them, and began blacking out every sentence with Yussef's name in it. It seemed like one way to regain control of my destiny. Or escape it, which would be about the same. No matter how many times I crossed them out, the letters were still visible. I pressed harder. I thought of Solange, the groove in her tongue when she took the nipple, a few white drops beading at the edge of her lips . . .

The sound of hands clapping made me jump. There were only three people left standing in front of the librarian. I smartly tore out the final pages of the pamphlet. The paper offered no resistance. Now I was ripping the pages to shreds, as if my life depended on destroying this document. There was a pile of little squares in my lap. After all, the original request was in Colin B.'s name; not much could happen to me. I stood up, shreds fell around my feet. As I walked by the encyclopedias, I slipped what was left of the pamphlet between two volumes. The librarian was checking in the last reader's materials, and from the size of the pile I could tell that it would take her a while to realize I was gone. A man in a gray smock stood at the exit. I walked toward him and stuck my hands in the air to show that they were empty. I immediately regretted the gesture—isn't a show of innocence tantamount to an admission of guilt? I tried to disguise my initial meaning with more miming, gesturing that it was raining, for instance, my index fingers pointing to the sky as if to say there was nothing to be done about it, palms pivoting to say that was that. The man glanced at the ceiling, looked at me dubiously, and as my arms still waggled idiotically above my head, he gave me the kind of indulgent smile doctors usually reserve for patients with incurable diseases. I forced myself to strike a more natural pose. My hands slid down the sides of my body. Yes, I was a dead man (grimace), I'd known that for a long time (one step forward), and I was pretending I didn't. I shrugged my shoulders, he stepped back, as if to size up how serious the offense was, then blocked my way. His gray smock, unbuttoned, showed the open neck of his mesh polo shirt, blond hairs, a silvery chain. His beer belly shrank from contact with me. Then I watched, a helpless spectator, as his hand came out of his waistband and ever so slowly clamped on my left shoulder. He wasn't going to let me out. I glanced toward the research librarian. She was looking for something in a box on the floor. You could only see the curve of her back above her desk, between the piles of books. The last patron faced us. The man began to frisk me, his fingers precise yet delicate. It was a professional search, I felt my face relax, felt inclined to cooperate. I produced my memo pad from my jacket. He flipped through it to check that no documents were concealed inside. A little square of paper flew down onto the tip of his shoe. The confetti was getting loose. I was dripping with sweat, trembling with fear or desire, I wasn't sure which. I suddenly saw what subtle delight Solange must have gotten from obeying me. Responding to my desires was appropriating them in a way, possessing me as fully as I possessed her. It surprised me to find myself envying her position. The constraints I placed on her day after day, on top of the yoke of captivity, may have been the foundation of an existence freed from doubt, and thus from anxiety.

The man in the gray smock asked me very politely to leave. Everything in the way I acted had been meant to arouse his suspicion, make him accuse me, have me make restitution, everything— and now he was letting me go, like a thief. Why didn't anyone ever give me a chance to defend myself? My act was no ordinary vandalism, I would have liked to explain that to him. I had just discovered the story of Yussef, my story, and once again I would find myself alone, with no one to talk to . . .

I walked slowly down the steps. In the street, people scurried along, their eyes on their feet. It was still raining. I didn't notice right away that someone was following me. Feeling sick again with guilt and the fear of punishment, I stumbled into a bus. A leather-gloved hand stuck a ticket in the stamping slot, just after mine. A strong odor of black tobacco wafted in the damp air. No need to turn around: it was clearly Colin B. I had no desire to start a conversation with him, yet his presence comforted me. Better than any words, the two rapid clicks of the ticket machine established a secret complicity between us. I made my way to the back of the bus, determined to find us seats, preferably back to back. Freezing droplets seeped from my hair onto the wet wool of my scarf. I took out my tube of vitamin C tablets. Crunching nervously on my last three tablets, I thought of the demoiselle crane with its makeshift prosthesis, the head keeper's black bicycle, Lisa's mother.

I sat across from an old man, by the window, leaving Colin B. the forward-facing seat in front. So in a twisted way, he was ahead of me without ever passing me.

Colin B. stood up when I buzzed for my stop. I had dozed all the way to Place de la Nation, and I didn't have the strength to force an encounter. I got off, slouching beneath my collar, and walked decisively toward the side entrance to the Zoo. The rain had stopped. The prostitute who worked the Avenue Daumesnil corner gave me a big smile. She had lost her heart to a squirmy little dog with eyes like a dead fish; it evidently shielded her from the disgust she felt toward the human race. My connection to the marvelous world of the Zoo, behind the iron gates, must have made me seem special to her, because no matter how unpleasant I acted, she still displayed a naive admiration for me, like a little girl who dreams of being a veterinarian when she grows up. That evening she clutched the dog inside the plunging neckline of her coat. He plastered her with ratty kisses, licked her neck, nipped at her ears, and she laughed. Colin B. was still fol-

lowing me. I heard his shuffling gait. His feet m
have been soaked from walking through puddles.
my indifference excited him, I confess that his pe
sistence was not without an effect on me. I tol
myself it was a little late to stop things now,
wouldn't have the nerve to slam the gate in his face.
Hadn't he bought me lunch? Courtesy was my
rationale for something that had started as simple
curiosity but had quickly become a certain form of
desire. All my life I had kept to myself and
watched, and now for once I was about to submit to
someone else's demands, as Solange had done to
her death.

In this frame of mind, I led Colin B. behind the
big boulder. This huge hollow structure had
become one of my favorite haunts since the change
in management. The viewing platform on top had
now been closed to the public for safety reasons,
which finally made it a decent place to go. Moss
was creeping over the cement, birds had nested in
the arch above the stairway, and two gray mounted
telescopes stood on one leg each, lost in mutual
contemplation. The elevator up to the terrace was
still in working order, though used only occasionally to reach the inner storerooms—the staff
preferred the service elevators. I went inside, turning my back to Colin B.; I didn't have the heart to
look him in the eye. I heard the wooden brace
slide into place. He lit a cigarette.

The old elevator started with an awful cre

At any moment it might break down, leaving us stranded two hundred feet off the ground, imprisoned inside a huge block of imitation stone—a scenario that heightened my sensations even further. I thought of Solange, enclosed in her iron tomb; then Colin B. undid his fly and pressed against me. He muttered something that sounded like a prayer. Anonymity had reduced him to a kind of giant insect, obtuse and obsessive, rubbing its genitals against my buttocks. Luckily there was the elevator, with its jerking halts, earsplitting noise, and the light that went off between each landing. I kept my index finger on the control panel, starting the machinery in motion over and over almost in spite of myself; the movement of the elevator excited me more than anything. Colin B.'s enigmatic patter filtered into my ears, bringing me back to reality the way an intravenous drip brings an intensive care patient back to life. He was parsimonious with his passion, going too far yet not far enough—farther than what was decent, but not enough to move beyond reason. Now he was asking, begging me to touch him, and his pleading began to annoy me. Yet I stood there without moving, even let him undo my belt. He tried to penetrate me, first with his gloved thumb, pressing his palm flat between my thighs; I contracted my muscles with all my might to stop him. Then, I don't know why, perhaps at the touch of his lips on my neck, my throat went tight with fear. I groped him

like a touchstone and I began to stroke wildly. It felt strangely exciting not to see, for once.

The elevator lurched to a halt. Colin B. lost his balance and fell hard against me. My head bumped the control panel. I screamed. Instinctively, I wiped my forehead with my hand. I must have cut myself just under the eyebrow. Colin B. leaned into me, I sensed he was ejaculating. His organ writhed between my buttocks again. Drops of blood ran down my nose, I was suffocating, the elevator went dark, I was going to black out, like when Solange died, the head keeper's arms stretched out to catch me, Lisa's mother's arms, and I held tight, clung to the brace so I wouldn't fall . . . Colin B. clutched at me, his panting silence pierced my eardrums. He was going to kill me, blood was dripping into my mouth. On the farm, when mice gorged on poisoned grain, they often found their way up to die on the rug in my room, dancing tipsily on their little hind legs until they dropped from exhaustion. I closed my eyes. The taste of blood in my mouth . . . I was twelve years old again, lying on a big white bed to have my tonsils removed, the doctor looming over me. It was Pierre-Jean, my foster mother's cousin by marriage, whom we often consulted because he didn't charge us. Why did that ludicrous detail stick in my memory? "No, no, it's all in the family," he would tell her when she made noises about paying him. The same words were repeated at each office visit, in the same gently scolding tone. And forget about having me go to the hospital for such a simple procedure. A lot was forgotten.

From the time I was seven, I had recurrent sore throats, developing into bronchitis. After five years of compresses, gargles, antibiotics, and inhalants, Pierre-Jean finally decided my tonsils should come out. My father had signed a release, so nothing stood in the way of executing what was first only a plan—today I would say a plot—featuring me as both beneficiary and victim.

Mèrade had gone directly into her cousin's consultation room and left me alone in the waiting room. The walls were covered with old engravings tracing the history of medicine. Their gilded frames, the rich display, fascinated me. I felt good, both overstimulated and slightly drowsy. Muffled laughter reached me from the next room. I glanced absent-mindedly at the pictures until one caught my attention. It was a print by someone called Boilly, dated 1827—honestly—with two panels representing excision of the uvula. I looked closer. The first tableau showed a hook-nosed doctor brandishing a syringe in hot pursuit of a half-naked man; a crowd of fellow physicians cheered him on. The rustic, jovial setting made the instrument seem even more menacing. The doctor gripped it in both hands, like an old-fashioned insect sprayer. The patient clutched a tasseled cushion to his buttocks. Two vicious male nurses perched on a tree branch above him, waiting to throw a sack over his head. Blind with fear, he suspected nothing. A little farther along, a rope stretched a few inches above the ground would trip him into a pile of straw, at the mercy of the medical profession.

The second panel showed him sprawled in a chair, his face puffy, head lolling backward. His neck was three fat, hairy folds between his head and the collar of his shirt. A caption quoted Ambroise Paré as saying that the uvula was the source of many *inconveniences*. When it grew elongated and enlarged, he advised, the prudent course was removal. Despite the satisfied smile on the doctor's face, I was not so sure of the outcome. The convalescent wore the blank, resigned expression of a steer led to slaughter.

The central section of the picture was a technical description of the operation. There was an enlarged view of the oral cavity. Staked out by teeth, it looked like a terrifying cavern. The offending nub of flesh dangled miserably at the back of the palate. The tonsils, also destined for extraction, were designated by two arrows on either side of the tongue. They were rather vague and insignificant-looking. More than the glands themselves, the typography of the words "Palatine Tonsils" impressed me. The downstroke of the P, the loops of the t's and l's in the old-fashioned writing were full as money pouches. The thought of their amputation filled me with unspeakable dread. Next to the gaping mouth was a drawing of "Castellan's snare," a strange object that looked like a cross between a dessert fork and a guillotine.

By now I was having a hard time swallowing. With no handkerchief available, I methodically spit my thick, stringy saliva into an ashtray I found on the radiator. I watched it fill like a tuberculosis patient reading his death warrant. I had the distinct impression they were hiding something from me. Hadn't the cousin said he would perform the operation in his consultation room? I imagined a windowless cubbyhole behind his desk, and in place of the engravings a collection of glinting scalpels. I would be bound to the chair, spread-eagled, with anesthesia that smelled like pine disinfectant held under my nose. It was awful. I was caught between two conflicting needs: on one hand, I had to get rid of this soft tissue threatening to swell until I suffocated, and on the other I wished to remain whole, in full possession of my defenses, even if they might be the source of *inconveniences*, as Ambroise Paré said in the caption. I hurled myself at the double doors separating the office from the waiting room. The partition was covered with a rust-colored curtain, and despite the thickness of the fabric I could hear Pierre-Jean's deep voice. The disjointed nature of the muffled sounds was far from reassuring. What were they plotting? The door was locked. I knocked, softly at first, perhaps in hope of overhearing some secret, then louder and louder. I peeped through the keyhole, but saw only a dark, moving mass. The doctor soon came to open the door for me, so cool it left me speechless. I'd straightened up too fast, knocked my forehead on the porcelain doorknob; my head was spinning and my feet didn't seem to be touching the ground, an unpleasant sensation. I clutched desperately at the curtain. Pierre-Jean came up to me, his wide body blocking out the room; he grabbed my arm and slapped me. I think he picked me up and carried me to the big white bed, without a pillow or blanket, at the other end of the apartment. We went through the consultation room, then down a long corridor with any number of doors. Mèrade appeared from nowhere, then disappeared. I woke up in the master bedroom at the farm. On the night stand, floating on the surface of a jar of slimy liquid, were two pink almond-shaped globs of flesh. I tried to call out. That taste of blood in my mouth . . .

The elevator started again. I opened my eyes just in time to see the light go out. Pain tore through my throat. Colin B. had untied my scarf and slid his thumbs beneath the damp wool. He still had his leather gloves on, his caresses were heavy, compressed. A fit of coughing came over me, and, curiously, made me feel better. Something had snapped inside my skull, the sick feeling vanished as suddenly as it had started. I eased my grip on the cross-brace and groped for the ground floor button. I was going to turn around, I had to turn around. My pants were sliding slowly down my legs. The feeling of helplessness was unpleasant, very unpleasant. I wanted to pull them back up, but Colin B. wouldn't let me. Letting go of my neck, he knelt and put his arms around me. I imagined Glibett fighting Beethoven for Solange. What was left of that boy pounding on the doctor's door, his throat on fire? The lights blinked. The back of my sleeve was red with blood. Where had I read that a razor blade, used correctly, can slice through the skin yet cause no more pain than a pinprick? Glibett, Solange, Mèrade, Pierre-Jean . . . I might black out again. I turned around, felt my organ brush against Colin B.'s face, then poke between his lips, glide on his tongue, bump against his palate. I felt his throat sucking me in. I was about to let go in him when a stupid question occurred to me: did Colin B. have his tonsils out?

Free fall, downfall. Forced withdrawal . . . I had an instant vision of Castellan's snare, the gloating face of the doctor in the old engraving, the syringe, the spiky teeth around the inflamed uvula, Glibett strutting like a war casualty in his Sunday best, Jeanne's stockings and her hand stuck between the blind slats, my Solange's tail whacking Beethoven's puckered chops, the Director in the studio rocking on his shooting-stick and me hiding behind the curtain, yes, me, watching . . . I was finally about to come when a familiar sound, like the memory of a rake scraping through gravel, sent me reeling back into that nether state of pleasure where nothing— nothing, ever—happens. Colin B. was rattling his tin of breath mints. A smell of licorice . . . His hand came closer, holding three tiny black squares out to me. When exactly had he taken his leather gloves off? He was begging me to suck the candies in front of him, "Suck them," he kept saying. His middle fin- ger was bent backwards, crooked, shaking with unbearable tremors. I saw him at noon, in the Tunisian restaurant, panting at the sight of the cous- cous he made me eat. Colin B., his bitten, nicotine- stained nails, looking like an Indochina veteran, Hollywood-style; Colin B. exhibiting his raised scars on the sidewalk. He stood up unsteadily, grip- ping my scarf, which he then wound around his neck as well, as if to bind us together forever, with a ring of red wool.

"You . . . you've hurt yourself," he stammered, languorously bringing his mouth close to mine. He was rattling the candies, his gums were streaked with white secretions: he spluttered that if I was good he would take care of me, good care of me, he liked me, or some such thing. His breath stank. He tried to kiss me. I felt Malcolm's fangs dig into my neck. "Scum," I shrieked, struggling for words, "you old bastard," but my pathetic insults only egged him on. His ugliness was stunning. I told him to go jerk off in church, at least he'd have the confessional curtain to wipe up his messes. I was horrible. I could have accused him of every vice in the book and he wouldn't have smiled at me any less lustfully. "Now, now," he said throatily, "there we are, there we are." I broke away from his hateful embrace, grabbed both ends of the scarf, and brought them around his neck. He pulled away, but that only tightened the noose. He was strangling. With all my weight I pushed him back against the wall. His lips moved, a hissing sound came out in spurts, then his lower jaw dropped in a frightful grimace. He stared at me with a stupid look on his face, eyes popping, only his Adam's apple was still moving, I felt it rise and fall, it defied me. My thumbs pressed the two sides of it together, held it too long, held on despite the convulsions, it endured forever, finally I felt it slide down into the trachea. It felt like wringing a rumpled towel, a purplish dishrag. A big orange slug was about to slip from his mouth. But all that could escape from those lips, chapped from the words they never dared say straight, those lustful lips, was a slobbery soul. The tin of breath mints fell on the floor and rolled to the door. I kicked it over the edge. I was strangling Colin B., the only witness to my misconduct.

It was so simple to get rid of the past. A roll, a fall, a thud. The throes of death and the silence of the Zoo at night. Solange, Glibett, and now Colin B., the list was getting longer. I ejaculated.

# 8

Form-fitting Italian leggings were all the rage that spring. Atir wore a pair under his jellaba. Geoffroy Saint-Hilaire made him a gift of some nearly new patent-leather pumps. The great scholar had not hesitated to leave the dusty silence of his office in the Paris Museum of Natural History, meet the giraffe in Marseilles, and head the expedition bringing her to King Charles X, her new master. The initial plan was to travel by boat to Le Havre, then inland down the canal system, but being no sailor, Geoffroy Saint-Hilaire argued that the shortest route between two points was always a straight line. The giraffe's successful program of daily outings proved she would be perfectly capable of crossing France on her own four feet. It was, furthermore, the most popular solution—and the least costly.

Aix, Lambesc, Orgon. . . The Count of Villeneuve-Bargemont had presented his guest with a superb, jeweled-studded leather collar. It had six braided tethers and a waterproof hood embossed with the coat of arms of France. Hassan led the march, followed closely by the three dairy cows that set the pace. Next came Yussef and Atir, handling the leads, gripping them like the ropes of a circus tent about to be blown away. At each major stopping point, a fresh team of four gendarmes signed on, wearing cocked hats and white gauntlets. The hoi polloi would gather at the city gates to greet the travelers. Yussef would reluctantly unfasten the giraffe's mantle, Atir would slip on his patent-leather pumps, and Geoffroy Saint-Hilaire would whip off the covering, which fell to the ground. Her marbled coat came into focus, an abstract landscape with a church or town hall for a foil. Everyone applauded, as if at the dedication of a monument. Yussef disliked this shameless cheering. The young giraffe—having just polished off an afternoon snack of two gallons of milk—surveyed the hubbub coolly. The puny no-neck humans clustering at her feet did not seem aware of the pointlessness of their milling about. Only Yussef remained perfectly still during the ceremony, both hands resting on the head of his bleached bone, legs spread, an imperturbable bodyguard. Geoffroy Saint-Hilaire would take advantage of the general goodwill and whisper a few outraged remarks to the mayor or his assistants about the disastrous state of the post houses in their district. The food was bad, the prices exorbitant, the mattresses crawling with fleas and bedbugs. . . The sympathetic officials sometimes invited him to dine, more rarely to stay overnight. This distinguished fifty-five-year-old scientist made them slightly uneasy, like a circus lion tamer or other animal handlers. Atir, on the other hand, found a warm welcome from the female population. White Horse Inn, Red Hat Hotel. . . He experienced the intoxication of petticoats hastily raised between two doorways, quick, quick, the fear of being discovered, the pleasure of discovering. He would doze off wherever he fell, exhausted, his tight Italian drawers around his ankles.

How long did I lie there with Colin B.'s corpse? My watch crystal had been shattered in the scuffle. The night was cold. I had dreamed about my tonsil operation. I could picture myself in the double bed in the master bedroom, just after my temperature had been taken. Why had Mèrade left the window open? I was shivering. No, I hadn't killed Colin B., he was the one who had jumped me like a mad dog. Self-defense. Don't think anymore. Once a tonsillectomy is performed, the site of infection disappears. Forget. I curled up against his body like a lost child, pulling the quilt over my head. Where was I? In the grip of pain, I couldn't even cry out. I felt too weak to get up. I heard Mèrade putting the dishes away in the kitchen, banging the pots and pans, moving the chairs, filling a pail with water, dumping it on the tile floor and mopping, knocking into the buffet, the table legs, the water heater, scouring until I thought my head would burst. What was so dirty in our life to make her scrub like mad every morning, deaf to the world around her, absorbed in the minutest task, the slightest variation in the external order of things?

It was the first time I had formulated the question in those terms. Yet it seemed I had always known the answer: it was better to try to do everything right than to be punished for something wrong. Where had I learned that? From the time I was very young, I had built up a solid wall to protect me from blame. The family debts were heavy: my mother's death, my father's late support payments, his stubborn refusal to remember my birthday or when to pick me up for vacation. It seemed normal to me to pay their debts. I did so conscientiously, and not without a certain pride. Learning to do farm chores wasn't the least of the hardships I made myself endure. The motions I went through every day after school only proceeded smoothly once I learned to think of them as the basis of my peace of mind, hard-won through continual penance. These small victories over myself nourished me, for lack of anything better. There was little room for tenderness in my foster family, no light touch, I had seen that from the first day there. The constant obsession with cleanliness was one more indication that you should leave nothing behind, no kiss, hug, or anything else that might open the door to sentiment—or resentment. My only escape route had been through illness, bronchitis, strep throat, head colds, laryngitis, every possible combination of respiratory infection. Only then could I let someone care for me. I loved those warm times, Mèrade's strong smell when she bent down to plump my pillows, the artificial banana flavor of the cough syrup, the way the mustard plasters burned.

And now a simple tonsillectomy would deprive me of these arousing interludes. Pierre-Jean was categorical: there would be no more strep.

Huddled under the covers, throat on fire, I quietly played with myself, pondering this sad outcome, when Mèrade's voice startled me. My hands instinctively flew to the pillow, on either side of my head. She asked me what I was "up to." I couldn't speak. My bouts of tonsillitis were over. Twelve years old, and no way out now.

There was a full year of follow-up before the operation could be pronounced a success. Despite a harsh winter, wet spring, beastly last half of August, despite even an Indian summer—you never know how warmly to dress—all I got was the occasional stuffy nose. Mèrade suffered from my new-found health as much as I did. What excuse did she have now for visiting her cousin Pierre-Jean? She became rash, studiously neglecting to light the space heater in my room, inviting a good case of the flu that would require medical attention. As soon as I showed the slightest fatigue, she clucked over my health. But no matter, I was really cured. I may still have been a sullen, sickly-looking child, small for my age, but that wasn't enough to send me to the doctor every week. I learned to make the most of early symptoms—dizziness, flushed skin, tingling sensations—without ever actually getting sick. This improved my status within the family to some extent.

Mèrade wasn't fooled, but she couldn't help hoping. Conventional in her own way, she could not conceive of adulterous relations without a legitimate excuse, and hoped I would eventually founder. I think my mute accusations frightened her more than her husband's childish blustering. Toward the end, I got a sick pleasure out of scaring her. I would sit across from her while she was shelling beans, cross my arms on the table, and stare at her. Or I would stand in front of the bathroom ventilator while she was showering and use a little pocket mirror to beam light in at her, the next best thing to invading her privacy with my own eyes. She was very religious, and I was sure that she saw these rays as the finger of God, personally pointing at her. Sometimes if I got down on the floor I could catch a glimpse of leg under the door, at best a flash of thigh. I was already intrigued by bodies in pieces. Mèrade always wore oversized dresses, layered with aprons, shawls, thick socks. This propensity for concealment excited my imagination. I hated her.

What can I say about my foster father? He operated in a different sphere, I sometimes wondered if we even belonged to the same species. That was the extent of my curiosity.

I awoke at daybreak, for real this time, huddled in one corner of the elevator. The blood on my face had dried, I had trouble opening my left eye. Colin B. lay still beside me. I would gladly have left him there, to rot, "as is," the tag line that farm equipment salesmen used for old milking machines. I no doubt felt I had already done my penance during my childhood, which eased my conscience. However, I decided it would be safer to dispose of the body before the Zoo opened. The best way would be to cut him up and stash him in the basement meat lockers, then sneak him out piece by piece. I would take my place in the great tradition of chain-saw murders that had regularly fueled conversation on the farm. The thought made me smile. I pictured myself at seventeen again, roaming the vast main hall of the Gare St. Lazare, from the war memorial to the snack bar, the snack bar to the lockers, empty suitcase in hand . . .

Why dwell on the past? Colin B. lay still at my feet, I was cold, I wanted to get it over with as quickly as possible. All that was left of me was a structure of crumbling stone. The woodwork was worm-eaten, the flooring warped, the plaster in the ceiling full of cracks. It was time to strip away the last shreds of wallpaper and live in the open, finally free of the continual need for justification. My father was dead, what need did I have to lie to myself? I was not like the daring criminals I read about as a teenager. I wasn't that good, I would never make the headlines. Besides, I had no desire to, I preferred to stay in the background. I fell limply into the category of cowards who left their victims behind a fence in a vacant lot. I was no trunk murderer, or even a murderer at all, despite appearances. I had only one excuse: Solange was dead and her absence haunted me. Day after day I fought to overcome the emptiness she had left behind, stuffing it with everything I could, memories, quirks, obsessions, like old newspapers crammed in a wet shoe to keep it from losing shape. I existed only in relation to that hollow inside, and even discovering Geoffroy Saint-Hilaire's letters wasn't enough to help me break out of this vicious circle. Except now Colin B.'s death had paid the debt still tying me to Solange. After six years of passive mourning, I finally felt I was back in action, reclaiming my power.

I knew of a storage loft inside the big boulder where nobody went, ever. Off-limits for safety reasons, only the vultures used it. The hardest part was getting Colin B. out of the elevator. My scarf caught in the cross-braces and I had an awful time getting loose. Finally I dragged him into the storeroom and locked it up tight. I heard wings flapping, screeches, I even thought I heard a human sound, though it wasn't possible—a peal of hysterical laughter that stopped dead. Behind the door, the big carrion-eaters would soon be fighting over the choice tidbits. I walked unsteadily up the steps leading to the platform on top of the boulder. The walls were covered with graffiti, dates, initials, lots of hearts with arrows through them, a few obscene drawings. "Like big pricks? Look for Pat, Lions' Den, Tuesdays," one inscription in the stairway read. M. loves M., and vice-versa. Agnes, Dani, Caroline, Valerie were here, 5/12/7?. Each of them, in their own way, felt the need to proclaim their existence, their desires, as if to keep death and its ghastly hoard at bay. I found myself smiling at these naive inscriptions. I felt light, almost too light. I had quietly settled my accounts, I no longer owed anyone anything. I belonged to the walking wounded, born of death pangs, reeling forward through the past. My only course was to follow in the footsteps of Yussef, keeper of the Pasha of Egypt's giraffe, beyond prejudice, finally faithful to my double calling. Was Lisa's mother aware of the world around her as she cared for her infant?

The cool air did me good. Paris was damp and tired at daybreak, a frumpy old thing rising from the earth like a grayish sand castle. The park was empty. The prostitute on the corner of the Avenue Daumesnil had gone home to sleep with her ratty little dog, its eyes like dead fish. In a few hours, the Zoo would open again. The head zookeeper would go on his daily rounds for the last time before his retirement. Whole classes of children would stop by the vulture's aviary, right next to the old ticket booth where Jeanne, the Director's Jane, used to sit. The satisfied vultures would huddle in the branches. I swore I wouldn't return to the spot where Colin B. was already starting to decompose. I had had the presence of mind to empty his pockets back in the elevator. I was quite proud of myself. For an amateur, I was handling things pretty well.

When I got to my hotel, everyone was still sleeping. I crept up to my floor, cleaned my wound, and collapsed on the bed. I was awakened by the chambermaid, amazed to find me in my room at two in the afternoon. I told her I was sick, to make her leave me alone, and the minute I said it I realized it was true. I had a terrible sore throat. Instead of heading for my well-stocked medicine cabinet, I opened the window and got back in bed. For the first time since my tonsils came out, I was going to get a good case of strep.

By dark I had a temperature of a hundred and three and the feeling it might go higher. All afternoon I had dreamed of Geoffroy Saint-Hilaire's letters, blurred with the ones I sent my father. The idea of writing Yussef's biography came to me. Wasn't I the sole trustee of his story? It had been left to me, and it was my duty to take up where the painter at the Zoo left off. I tried to get up and find my notebooks, but my head was spinning too fast. Panic-stricken, I called the desk and asked them to send for a doctor, pick any one of those emergency services from the business cards tacked up on the front-hall bulletin board. Twenty minutes later a solid-looking redhead bustled into my room. The way he yanked my shirt up, using the tips of his fingers, made me take an instant dislike to him. I hadn't eaten since the day before—since the cous-cous Colin B. bought me—and my stomach looked alarmingly hollow. I answered the doctor's questions with groans. I began staring him down, but he met my gaze with crushing detachment and studied my cut.

"We'll have to bandage that up for you," he said.

His forced smile, his briskness, his surly determination to help me, made me see how sinister I must look to him. I wanted to slap his face. What did he have that I didn't? Gabardine pants, permanent-press. A smell of aftershave, a clear conscience, unruffled even this late in the day, smugness to spare. With his black bag, he reminded me of the tractor mechanic who used to come to the farm. The doctor listened to my chest, then his plump hands reached toward my neck. I don't know what came over me, I jumped out of bed and cringed by the painting. Touching the canvas calmed me. The doctor froze for a second. He was talking, but I couldn't make out what he was telling me. I heard the word "ganglion" several times. He went out in the hall and called down to the desk clerk. While he was gone, I worked my way closer to the Pasha of Egypt's giraffe. The sweet warmth of her breath enfolded me. I recognized Solange's scent.

The fever transported me into a uniquely lucid state. A wealth of previously unseen details suddenly struck me; with the clear logic of dreams, they combined in a flash to give me a picture of everything around me. In one glance I saw the legs of my bed, the dust on the empty shelves, the pier in Marseilles, the memo book in my jacket pocket, and Joseph in Yussef, or Yussef inhabiting Joseph, in fact I saw myself as someone else, from both inside and out. History protected me. My heart was pounding so hard I could barely stand still. King Charles X's court painter begged me not to move. His red mane glistened in the setting sun. I struck Yussef's pose. He had certainly never had his tonsils out, that was the only difference between us. What if Geoffroy Saint-Hilaire discovered that we had switched places?

"Say ah, stick out your tongue, say ah . . . "

The professor was losing patience. I felt Yussef's turban wind around my head, my fingers clenched his makeshift sword. Khartoum, Cairo, Alexandria . . . the earth spun like a ball under my bare feet . . . Marseilles, Paris, Aix. Suddenly I spied the doctor plunging a syringe into a tube of transparent liquid. To make him feel better, I decided to act as if I hadn't noticed. "Ha, Ha!" I shouted. I egged him on, lowering my shorts, laughing at the thought of his needle hitting nothing but a thick coat of paint. "I like mashed potatoes," I finally said to break the tension in the air, "but I hate lumps." I was perfectly aware of how incoherent I sounded. He shouldn't worry about my weight, I've always looked like a drowned cat, I couldn't get anything down because of my throat, no use troubling His Majesty's cook. He nodded, serious as could be, and then I realized the doctor wasn't normal. Anyone in full possession of his mental faculties would have asked me what on earth I was babbling about. He only smiled at me.

"No mashed potatoes, I promise," he said, creeping toward the canvas.

Then I saw he was looking at me, at my organ. Ha, Ha! he blushed. I sensed he was close to the combustion point. Tractor mechanic, yes, it fit him to a tee. My ersatz mother would have said he had a screw loose. It was on account of her that I hated lumps. She stirred all her concoctions with a swift, decisive hand, very arousing. Coffee we never drank. Chicory, sometimes, thick as motor oil. I could have told that to the doctor, but was he really an M.D.? These days anyone might intercept a radio frequency on a portable telephone and turn up posing as a physician. Hadn't I been praised and consulted by the veterinarians at the Zoo?

The desk clerk got there just as the doctor was about to put his hand on my shoulder. This clerk was the chambermaid's husband, our relationship was strictly business. The only person worthy of notice in the place was the owner, but she and I were both so naturally reserved that our friendship never developed. She knew I paid my rent in cash on the fourth of every month, and asked no more of me. During my seven years at the hotel, I don't believe I had ever given her cause for complaint.

"Show this gentleman to the door," I ordered the clerk.

Draped in the folds of my jellaba, I could take on the world. My voice was strong and full. I heard someone calling me in the distance. "Yussef, Yussef!" Was it Atir? I would have liked to know what my rival's face looked like. Unfortunately, I had to leave the painting to hunt for a five-hundred-franc note and slip it into the bogus doctor's bag, over his protests. He tried to give me change. "Keep it, keep it," I insisted. It looked to me as if his stethoscope was dangling loose around his neck. I suggested he buy a new one. He seemed upset. I let him write his prescription and give me his shot: I was sorry for him. I saw the desk clerk motion that things weren't quite right in the head. I touched my fingers to my lips, hushing him. No reason to make the doctor feel any worse. If he knew we were on to him, the man might turn dangerous. "Yussef!" The voices called again. A hot, dry wind swept their words away. I slid under the covers. I heard the door close, and I slept. The other hunters had fallen behind. In a little grove of flowering mimosa, a very young Solange awaited me. Her mother's elongated neck emerged from the network of branches, nervous eyes scanning the horizon.

# 9

At last they arrived in Paris. Hassan, Atir and Yussef had to dress up like operetta Mamelukes to appear before King Charles X and present the giraffe. They were swathed in more Oriental drapery than they knew what to do with and fitted with pointed Turkish slippers. Atir managed to get his on over his patent-leather pumps. All the way from Marseilles to Paris they had brought him luck; he was not about to part with them so close to the official ceremony. For similar reasons, Yussef refused to surrender the leg bone he wore. Since the chief of protocol had asked him at least to keep it hidden in the folds of his costume, Yussef quietly sat on the ground in the middle of the carriageway. The giraffe, obeying his orders, posted herself behind the man who had become her master and friend. There they stayed.

The procession was due to get under way from the Jardin des Plantes at five o'clock in the morning. It was raining, the military escort was late, everyone's patience began to wear thin. The Museum scientists, the generals in plumed headgear were indignant. Hassan, hoping to relieve the tension, took a small cup and a pair of dice out of his pocket. He crouched down on his heels across from Yussef and started a round of *zhardoun*. The object of the game was to get the lowest score in nine throws. Shaking the dice, he complained of all the woes besetting him. Downpour, evil eye, chronic liver and fluid troubles . . . If heaven had any pity on his paltry existence, he would arrive at the gates of the Parc de Saint-Cloud and give up the ghost as he bowed to the royal family. Geoffroy Saint-Hilaire was hardly better off. Inability to void, inflammation of the urinary tract, the doctor gave him less than three hours on his feet before he landed in the hospital. The gossip was that Atir had gangrene, thus he never took off those shiny shoes. His feet were rotting, beyond help.

Hassan's voice disappeared into a thick cough, then surfaced again, thin and pathetic. He painted such a bleak picture of his travel companions that Yussef began to wonder if he didn't have something himself, a nameless sickness all the more deadly for having no particular symptoms. He saw the tibia crawling with beetles, the dried marrow between his brown thighs. That day had tipped the balance of his life. Hassan rolled the dice. Double sixes. He lost so consistently Yussef suspected him of cheating. The mounted escort had just arrived and was lining up along the Austerlitz bridge. Without a thought for the game going on at the feet of the giraffe, Geoffroy Saint-Hilaire gave the signal to depart. Atir grabbed the reins. Yussef jumped up and snatched them out of his hands. The startled giraffe looked at him, her head slowly bobbing. Atir hastily abandoned his post and took shelter in the skirts of a heavily decorated magistrate. The crowd of dignitaries followed the whirl of black herdsmen with a certain enjoyment. They felt they were finally experiencing a historic moment, complaining loudly when the chief of police intervened, less to protest against his brutality than to show they regretted being deprived of a fight that promised to go beyond the ordinary. The chief of protocol, overwhelmed, ran from one side of the square to the other swinging his silver-tipped cane. It had stopped raining. The procession got under way as the bells of St. Clotilde's rang out six o'clock.

The giraffe behaved like a real little lady. She ate the rose petals the Duchess of Berry offered, and repeatedly licked the king's wig. Geoffroy Saint-Hilaire answered all the courtiers' questions slowly and carefully, as if talking in his sleep. The last ten miles had nearly finished him. Yes, he was saying, the giraffe is the world's tallest mammal. No, as far as we can determine, it has no vocal cords, gallbladder, or tear ducts. Its brain accounts for only one-eight hundredth of its total weight. Yes, the name comes from *zarafa*, the Arabic for charming, pleasant one. No, it usually sleeps standing up. Yes, twenty years, they rarely live past the age of twenty . . .

At these words, there was a collective gasp. Only the lanky Duchess of Angoulême seemed unmoved by this cruel and unusual fate. Yussef didn't understand why she was looking at him so deliberately. Was someone talking about him? Then Yussef noticed the rip in his Turkish trousers, and the tip of the tibia poking out. On the way back to town, he was given a thousand francs on the king's behalf. And so the journey ended.

How to relive that flash of lucidity, that moment of absolute happiness in the grip of fever when I saved the baby giraffe from Atir's bloody saber? The chambermaid's husband looked stunned when he saw me leave the hotel that afternoon. Did he honestly think a mere sore throat could keep me from attending the head zookeeper's retirement party? Ha, ha! Little did he know. I even dug out a bottle-green dress suit my father had given me for my eighteenth birthday, and a new shirt. Catching a glimpse of my face in the hallway mirror, I was sorry I hadn't felt up to shaving. The doctor had bandaged my left eyebrow and daubed the dressing with yellowish liquid. I was still very tired despite the twelve hours of sleep that followed his visit. Cold gusted into the entryway when I opened the door. I buried my face in my red scarf, which after all this time was leaning more toward pink, though I always washed it myself, by hand.

I got to the Zoo restaurant just as the manager was bringing in the champagne. She asked me if I'd been hurt, and the question seemed so stupid I simply shrugged my shoulders. My grunt was drowned out in the general hubbub. I spotted Jeanne Blin, and her presence comforted me, in spite of everything. I walked up to thank her for coming, but she gave a surprised little smile when I spoke to her.

Was it possible she didn't recognize me? Thundering applause interrupted our reunion. I decided to ignore the cashier, since that was her wish. Some things about the past are better forgotten. I understood her attitude all too well, though I must confess it hurt me. Unaccustomed to wearing a suit, I felt a bit stiff in my jacket, and the shirt kept riding up uncomfortably over the top of the vest. Jeanne's skirt was black, her stockings much thicker than they used to be.

Everyone had chipped in to buy the head keeper a new bike, one of those sleek, lightweight racers, about as appropriate as a fingertip veil on a firefighter's helmet. One of the groundskeepers was discreetly passing between tables to collect the last few contributions. I thought I heard that he was still slightly shy of the total. He paused in front of me much longer than was reasonable, and since I didn't move a muscle he bent down to speak to me. I faked a coughing spell that sent him on his way. It was out of the question for me to associate myself with such a stupid purchase.

At one of the outdoor tables, the head keeper struggled with his huge package. He fumbled with the staples and ribbons, it wouldn't have occurred to anyone to help him. Finally, he freed his new mount from the box. They made him hop on and ride around a pile of chairs. He was ridiculous. Worse: he seemed happy. Performing bears sometimes wear the same kind of satisfied expression

when they parade under the big top on their span-
gled unicycles. If I'd had the courage to act, I
would have strangled him before he saw the absur-
dity of his gift. It was like giving the complete
works of Balzac to a terminal cancer patient. The
head zookeeper had been handed a death warrant,
I already knew it, he was going to disintegrate the
minute he had to surrender his uniform. How
could he survive the test of freedom? Nothing and
no one awaited him at home. I wished I could help
him.

Still, I raised my glass along with everyone
else when the staff delegate proposed a toast at the
end of his speech. My cowardice was matched
only by their obtuseness. The young lady who ran
the souvenir stand by the main entrance agreed to
sing a song that everyone ignored. The champagne
had the sweet taste of an events committee pur-
chase-in-bulk, and the snack mix blushing secre-
taries passed from group to group smelled moldy. A
few decorations had been tacked up for the occa-
sion. I wondered if, twenty-five years down the
line, they would be hypocritical enough to throw
such a party for me.

I sat at my usual table near the bay window
overlooking the giraffe exhibit. A great sadness
took hold of me. My powerlessness to help the
head keeper move on to his final trial made me
realize how vain my thoughts were. What use was
it to set myself apart from the affable herd of fellow

workers if I just went back to my hotel without even telling him that I wasn't fooled by the base charade? I suddenly saw that through him, they were getting rid of me. The Zoo was cleaning out its cages. In our different ways, we were the last vestiges of the old administration, reminders of the shooting-stick, the bow ties, everything arbitrary, superfluous. In the morning, nothing would be left of those days.

The head keeper was alone, standing on his makeshift platform, not sure what to do with his idle body, and I watched him from the other end of the room, alone as well, when a gray lump moved between us. I whisked out my glasses. The new director approached me with an outstretched hand. In the same instant, a voice rang out behind me.

"Yussef, Yussef," it kept saying.

I turned, but no one was there. It was not the first time since Solange's death that I had felt the presence of some strange force at my back. It usually happened at night, at the hotel. The new director looked at me intently. His fly was level with my eyes. The obvious suddenly hit me: I should resign. Wouldn't that be the best way to prove my sincere attachment to the head keeper? Unable to find words to express this surge of solidarity, I could only dump my glass on the new director's hand. The sparkling wine ran down his wrist, and as he waved his arm to call someone to help him, it leaked beneath the sleeve of his jacket. His assistant came running. Red-faced and spluttering with shame, he tried to hush up the scandal. I backed him toward the buffet and pushed him into a plate of lumpfish-and-sour-cream canapés. He got to his feet very slowly, the little smashed squares clinging to his chinos. The head keeper rushed over to protect me from the director's henchmen. Couldn't he see that I was the one defending him?

"Don't mind him," he was saying, "he's had too much to drink, I'll handle it, please."

Why did he have to insist I was drunk? I knew exactly what I was doing. I took off my glasses, resolving to confront my adversaries without them, my ludicrous but illusory magic shield. We shall see what we shall see, I told myself. After thirty-four years on the job, they were letting the head keeper go, like a clown who had stopped getting laughs. Out, they were shouting, to the junkyard with that old black bike! Who did they think they were fooling? An inebriated trainee hopelessly attempted to elbow his way through to me.

"Here's what you need," he yelled, waving a tin ladle, "just get him behind the knees with this!"

It was like an insane asylum. The room was overheated, I was dripping with sweat. The youngest employees rushed the buffet, sweeping away the last few peanuts. I got a squirt of mayonnaise on my forehead, my bandage came off. Still I remained stoic, the mayo stung my eyes, I thought about Colin B., Colon B. and his midnight oil, the prostitute's dog like something out of an oil slick.

The voice was still calling, "Yussef, Yussef." I restrained myself from ramming the whole crew with my head. No, they didn't deserve it. Yes-men, I thought to calm myself down, bunch of underpaid grovelers, pack of mongrel management watch-dogs, ready to fight for a pretzel and a cup of san-gría. "Ha, ha!" I said, slamming my fist into the head keeper's stomach. It was crucial that he not be seen as my accomplice, I alone was responsible for my actions. He fell, clutching his midsection, and I still don't know whether he was pretending or if I accidentally found the weak spot in his robust constitution. Twenty people surged forward to give him first aid, allowing me to escape to the back of the room. The overhead lights went out at the exact moment I was leaving. Startled by the darkness, I collided with the manager as she came out of the kitchen with the sheet cake and its sixty-five flicker-ing candles. The cake fell. A bluish flame sprang from the pile of napkins on the buffet table. I thought of Jeanne, the old Director's Jane, following this route into the restaurant almost fourteen years earlier, her stocking with a run in it, her floppy bosom squeezed into her lacy brassière.

I latched the door behind me. The tabby cat dozed by the refrigerator. He opened an eye, his lit-tle pink nose quivered at the smell of smoke. He leaped out of his basket and followed me outside. I wondered if animals were allowed inside correc-tional facilities. There, at least, you would be accepted as you were, without respect to age, sex, or ability. For life, if necessary.

My path led instinctively toward Solange's old pen. Something exploded behind me. I turned to look: the back room of the restaurant was on fire. I started to run. "Yussef, Yussef!". . . It was deep and full, a man's voice. What was I hoping when I slid the door to the pen open? How did I think for a single second that Solange would be there, that memory was stronger than time, stronger than death itself? In the darkness, I saw a huge rump come into focus, and I thought I recognized my darling, her odd way of shifting her weight from one foot to the other as she chewed her cud, her flank to the wall. Her coat would quiver, like before, beneath my fingertips. "Solange," I whispered, "my sweetheart, my silent beauty." Sometimes, she would pretend not to hear me, and her elfin humor delighted me. I wanted to press my mouth to the damp flesh of her nostrils, I would only need to climb up into the hayloft, swing open the trap door, and her lips would seek me out, her agile tongue searching for the saltiest patches of my skin. I was so overwhelmed that I froze, barely daring to breathe, I was too afraid she would vanish again, my beauty.

Then a sound came to shatter my dream. At first it seemed like no more than the squeak of a mouse. Then it continued, grating, steady: a giraffe grinding its teeth. A smell grabbed at my throat, an odor of stale urine. Solange had smelled of sour milk and dead leaves. I could have picked her scent out among a thousand others, with my eyes closed, it was so particular. I turned on the lights. My eyes came to rest on something tall, with a sort of stick-shaped gland on the underbelly. Beethoven! I reached my hand out toward him. And what if he let me touch him? I had no time to consider how absurd my gesture was. Beethoven bucked. I clung to the wall. His hooves banged furiously against the bars of the cage. Protected by the radiator, I couldn't help taking my thing out, as if to compare it to his, man to man, and see who could piss the farthest, who could shoot off first. His impatience excited me. I won. My sperm disappeared into the fresh straw. I took it as the sign of a great change. Not only because I'd been able to come without the terrifying feeling of being outside myself, a twitch-ing, disjointed marionette, but also because I hadn't needed to imagine a whole setting other than the one I was in, right there at that moment, thinking about Solange. No cameo appearances by Mèrade, Malcolm, Jane, Glibett, Lisa, or Colin B., his droop-ing neck, Colin B. and his damned breath mints. It felt like a turning point: no more umbrella handles to aim, jiggle, slide, press, insert, retract. To hell with train and subway platforms, the lines, the bus-tle, gloved hands, packed buses: I loved Solange.

And I love her, I finally dare to love her.

I had shut my eyes, savoring my happiness. I'm not sure how reality reclaimed its rightful place. At any rate, when I opened them again, Beethoven was leaping out of the cage. Ha! Ha! The wretch, far be it from me to hold him back, he had no business in Solange's private pen. No one had even thought to ask me, evidently. The other giraffe people were doing things behind my back since the Director left, getting even, jerking me around, but they'd see . . . Joseph can look out for himself. For all I cared, Beethoven could get run over by a truck, impale himself on the spikes on one of the gates, slip on the asphalt and break his back. I hated the lummox, his conceited sneer, his whole gangly harem. Giraffes in captivity are senseless contraptions, Solange was commendable for putting up with them. They defy the most elementary rules of logic, they barely qualify as living creatures, only as a walking paradox— a paradox unaware. The Creator must have been fooling around with leftover parts, what other explanation could there be for such an aberration? Thank the Lord, as Colin B. might say, He passed out, dead drunk, before He had time to finish their horns and give them a voice. Who knows what plaintive wail they might have ended up with?

Solange was so different. I admired her patience. I don't say that out of jealousy. Observing Beethoven quickly revealed from what depths of stupidity this antediluvian blob operated. If only his vanity hadn't made him even sillier than he was to begin with, I could have forgiven him. But no. He watched the world from a height of fifteen feet with such arrogance that it was impossible to detect the slightest glimmer of anything vaguely resembling intelligence. He was still trying to get through the small door in the hallway behind the holding pens, his front feet splayed seventy degrees, rump wedged in the opening, while I had just thrown open the exit giving him direct access to the main pathway through the Zoo. I could call him all I wanted, he stayed put, his organ straining for release, trembling with desire, so aroused he would have settled for mounting a fly. He didn't even move when the fire engine sirens started. The blaze must have spread from the kitchen. Honestly, Beethoven was deaf as a post. I had to stand in front of him waving my arms until he finally turned around and escaped out the main door. I turned to watch him hurtle into the restaurant's sidewalk tables, knocking them over, then jump over the shrubbery, frolicking like a colt to be let out to join his mother. He was magnificent in the firelight. His coat glowed with the amber highlights seen in new-born giraffes. Everyone was running in all directions, unsure whether it was more important to catch the loose animal, put out the fire, or run to safety. They were quite ridiculous. I seized the opportunity to slip out of the stables and head for the big boulder.

From the upper platform, two hundred feet off the ground, all the agitation looked even more ludicrous. I had climbed up the stairway, afraid I might rouse Colin B.'s spirit in the elevator. From floor to floor, the voice followed me. It said that Yussef was glad. "Yussef is glad," it parroted. I was finally out in the open. Beethoven was still galloping around, neck swaying, forelegs striding broadly. He looked like a boat caught in a storm. Instead of heading for the grounds, he kept making wide circles around the building, mesmerized by the fire, a pathetic dance. The fire fighters' helmets gleamed in the gathering dark. A group of men hurried toward the infirmary. I thought I spied the head keeper's new racing bike, abandoned near the sidewalk tables. Hadn't he left the old one, his father's, at the door to the restaurant? All the sirens went still at the same time. I slipped a coin into one of the telescopes, unwittingly interrupting their silent confabulation. Zoo visitors used to get a thrill out of locating from above what they had seen below, as if this new approach gave them entry to a tailor-made universe, all the more inviting for being out of focus, disjointed, and liable to disappear at any moment. Hands gripping the machine, rear ends sticking out, they clung to this fleeting image until the last possible moment. I understood them. I heard the coin clink. The lens opened. A recording started to spit out a scratchy commentary on the Paris Zoological Garden's forty-two acres of educational, recreational parkland. I shook the telescope. The voice wavered, stopped for a moment, then the speech started over in some unknown language. "Yussef," it creaked, "Yussef, Yussef!" I had barely spotted the entrance to the restaurant when I saw the head keeper dash into the flames. "Yussef!" He was calling me. Forgetting I was on top of the boulder, I ran after him. My right knee hit hard against the iron railing, knocking me backward onto the concrete, yet I clearly felt my body hit the ground, two hundred feet below. Pain kept me from realizing that something inside me had just died.

When I regained control of the periscope, it was already too late. Four men in fireproof suits were carrying the head keeper's body out on a stretcher. The cashier ran up to them. The way she froze a few feet shy made me see that it was over for him. With an accuracy that amazed me, I pointed the lens at Beethoven's rump. Wasn't he the only one to blame for this carnage? "The future of life on earth is uncertain," the recording whined, "and we provide a much-needed refuge for animals now endangered in the wild." A refuge for whom? The head keeper was dead. Tomorrow I would receive a registered letter terminating my employment and be put out in the cold like a dog. But wasn't I the only survivor of an endangered species? Beethoven still had his huge erection. I followed him, stride by stride, anticipating his movements like a hunter lin-

ing up his shot. I possessed him, as he had possessed my Solange, no, he would never escape from
me now. I was his master, the only guiding light in
his pitiful existence  His whole being yearned
toward me, something was going to happen, something irreversible that would link us forever . . .

Then Beethoven collapsed.

I couldn't get over it myself: at the exact moment I
willed it, he fell, with no obstacle in his path. I had
killed him. Killed him with a look. I swung the
periscope around to the crowd of Zoo employees.
The veterinarian appeared in the bushes with his
tranquilizer dart gun. A wave of panic swept over
the group. Now I had them, the true guilty parties.
Ha! Ha! They didn't deserve to live, but Yussef is no
criminal, you hear, Joseph is a bird, he sees the
whole world through the eye of a needle.  Lurking
in his dreams, Joseph understands.
    He looks, but suddenly everything is dark.
The coin has hit bottom, the curtain drops. They are
going to take us away to a dungeon. A blind-walled
cell, my Solange, protected by bars, where we will
finally be free again. Prison is our last refuge in this
beetle-infested world. They're coming up, Solange,
I feel my strength ebbing. A door slams, they're getting out of the elevator. I'll tell them I killed Colin
B., where to find his body. A body of evidence.
They'll  lock us up for the rest of our lives, and the

veterinarian will have to chain-saw Beethoven to pieces all by himself, like a Grade A railway trunk murderer.

They're getting closer, they're looking for us. Big beer drinkers, my Solange, your enemies, the ones who dragged you away from your native Africa, who killed the head keeper, yes, killed him with their twelve-speed bike and pudgy cold-reddened hands. Don't worry, love, these tears running down my cheeks are drops of blood, it's nothing, they'll never hurt me again. I will do whatever your sweet eyes command, obey you without a murmur, I will be your Joseph, son of Yussef, faithful and devoted guardian of our destiny. A long moonless night, far from the hue and cry, freed from the certainty of words. Let them put us on trial, throw me in jail. I will be mute at my sentencing. I don't owe anyone an explanation, I'm free, we're free, and if I can't live without seeing, can't resist the temptation to talk, I'll cut out my tongue, pluck out my eyes. From the shadows our love will shine bright, my Solange, our true love.

Paris went wild over the Egyptian Beauty. "Giraffe," "Savannah," and "Sudan Marble" were the new shades introduced at all the fashion houses. The neck was worn long, tied with a brick-red ribbon, the head accessorized with extravagant cake-topper ornaments, "giraffe style."

On Sundays, the middle classes no longer thronged to the Pont-Neuf for a free demonstration by the dog shearer, but instead lined up to pay admission at the Jardin des Plantes. More than six thousand visitors gazed in wonder. Then everyone forgot.

Atir and Hassan were sent back to their own country at the request of the British consul; consumed with jealousy, he was plotting to ship a hippopotamus to London. Yussef moved into a balcony above the giraffe's new quarters in the Orangerie. He slept in a hammock rigged twelve feet above the ground, his hand resting between two round, stubby horns. Like the giraffe, he lived on onions, grains, and milk. He left the Jardin des Plantes only three times a year: in the spring, he hired a carriage to Montmorency and paid for two hours of cherry picking, stuffing himself with fruit until he could eat no more. In early summer, when the heat began to build, he went for a dip in the Seine. Not knowing how to swim, he wrapped his ankles around a tree trunk and simply floated. In late September, he went to the Belle Jardinière department store and bought a certain cologne—for its long-necked flask—and four lengths of wool he used to make himself a jellaba exactly like last year's.

Only once did Yussef stray from the Botanical Gardens in winter. He learned that His Highness the Viceroy Mohammed-Ali had sent a new gift to France: an obelisk shipped up the Nile from Luxor, across the sea, and 540 miles upriver from Marseilles to Paris. It would land at the Quai de la Concorde on Wednesday, 23

December 1833. Yussef arrived Tuesday evening. He found a spot under the bridge and camped. It was the first time since his arrival in France that he had slept apart from his giraffe—though in fact neither one of them slept a wink that night. Finally, to the cheers of the crowd, the boat docked. Since Yussef had imagined that the obelisk was some fabulous beast from the Atlas mountains, he was most disappointed and decided never again to depart from his customary routine.

The giraffe died in 1845, at the age of twenty, out of favor. Yussef disappeared the same day, vanishing into thin air. No one worried. Years passed, then finally a renovation uncovered his bones in a hollow wall between the hayloft and the Orangerie. Also found were dice, a great many empty bottles, a few spools of black thread, and a monumental bone still to be seen at the Museum's Comparative Anatomy Department, tagged as the fifth tibia of the Pasha of Egypt's giraffe.